THE CARPENTER'S SON

Letters from Magdala

THE CARPENTER'S SON

Letters from Magdala

Brenton G. Yorgason and Richard G. Myers

Published by Covenant Communications, Inc.
American Fork, Utah

Printed in the United States of America
First Printing: October 1994

01 00 99 98 97 96 95   10 9 8 7 6 5 4 3

ISBN 1-55503-765-8

DEDICATION

We wish to dedicate this book to our fathers, Thomas G. Myers and J. Gayle Yorgason, whose unwavering examples of lifetimes of righteousness have consistently instilled within our hearts a love for, and testimony of, the carpenter's son.

ACKNOWLEDGMENTS

While numerous people have provided encouragement and direction in the formation of this story, we wish to especially thank Thomas G. Myers for his research and support, and Jason G. Yorgason for his "on location" insights into the Holy Land and the historical setting for this story. We also thank Lew and Marilyn Kofford, as well as Giles Florence and Valerie Holladay, for their timely insights, suggestions, and encouragement. And last, though certainly not least, we wish to thank our wives and most devoted fans, Margaret and Susie, for their reading, brainstorming, editing, and especially their constant love and support. They truly are the winds beneath our wings.

Historical Note

Many miles north of Jerusalem lies a small village in a hollow among the hills of Galilee. This village, for the past two thousand years, has been known to Christians as Nazareth. It is located just above the plain of Esdraelon, near the main roads of Palestine. It was in this quaint village that Joseph and Mary resided, and where, with the rest of their children, the boy Jesus spent his childhood—and in fact the first thirty years of his life.

The apostle Luke was the only record keeper to mention Christ's boyhood experience, wherein he states: "The child grew, and waxed strong in spirit, filled with wisdom: and the grace of God was upon him. And Jesus increased in wisdom and stature, and in favour with God and man" (Luke 2:40, 52).

The primary setting for our fictitious story of the youthful Jesus is the annual journey to Jerusalem for the Feast of the Passover. This feast is still celebrated today, in commemoration of the night—approximately 1,300 years before Christ's birth—when the angel of death passed over the doorsteps of the Israelites as they were about to be released from Egyptian captivity by the prophet Moses.

Again extracting from Luke 2:41-51, we find:

> Now his parents went to Jerusalem every year at the feast of the passover.
>
> And when he was twelve years old, they went up to Jerusalem after the custom of the feast.
>
> And when they had fulfilled the days, as they returned, the child Jesus tarried behind in Jerusalem; and Joseph and his mother knew not of it.
>
> But they, supposing him to have been in the company, went a day's journey; and they sought him among their kinsfolk and acquaintance.
>
> And when they found him not, they turned back again

to Jerusalem, seeking him.

And it came to pass, that after three days they found him in the temple, sitting in the midst of the doctors, both hearing them, and asking them questions.

And all that heard him were astonished at his understanding and answers.

And when they saw him, they were amazed: and his mother said unto him, Son, why hast thou thus dealt with us? behold, thy father and I have sought thee sorrowing.

And he said unto them, How is it that ye sought me? wist ye not that I must be about my Father's business?

And they understood not the saying which he spake unto them.

And he went down with them, and came to Nazareth, and was subject unto them: but his mother kept all these sayings in her heart.

From our reading of the four Gospels, we become well aware of six true and trusted friends of Jesus. The first of these was Mary Magdalene, who came from Magdala, a small village on the western shore of the Sea of Galilee, only fifteen miles east of Nazareth. This same Mary Magdalene was healed by Christ. She was also near the cross at the time of the crucifixion, was at Christ's burial, and was again at the tomb on the morning of the resurrection. Mary Magdalene, along with Mary, the sister of Martha and Lazarus, was the first to visit with the resurrected Christ.

These events identify three additional friends of Jesus, who perhaps knew him in his youth. These were the sisters, Mary and Martha, and their brother, Lazarus. We know from Luke's writings that *this* Mary sat at Jesus' feet. The apostle John then records that it was this Mary who sent for Jesus after the death of her brother, Lazarus; and then later, while hosting him in her home just prior to the crucifixion, anointed Jesus' feet with ointment, and then wiped his feet with her hair.

This same Mary was also with Mary Magdalene at the empty tomb that early Easter morning, and then later that morning first visited with the resurrected Lord. These two, along with Mary, the mother of our Lord, comprise the three Marys in Jesus' life.

The fifth friend, Joseph of Arimathaea, assisted the Savior at the conclusion of his life. He was a member of the powerful Sanhedrin council, which consisted of 71 members and was presided over by a high priest. This council was responsible for religious and civil functions of the Jews, under the close scrutiny of the ruling Roman empire. This council was abolished with the destruction of Jerusalem in 70 A.D. At the time of Christ, however, it was very much the Jewish power structure. Since Joseph of Arimathaea was a member, it was even more significant that he step out of the shadows and provide a final resting place, a tomb, for the crucified Savior of the world.

A sixth "friend," Simon of Cyrene, as recorded by Matthew, Mark and Luke, is the man who came forth from the crowd and carried the Savior's cross as the Son of Man pressed forward toward Golgotha and his own crucifixion. We have no historical account of Jesus meeting this man earlier than this, but the timely respite he provided the scourged and convicted Christ is sufficient for us to include him in our story.

Although history does not tell us when Jesus met these six trusted friends, for the purposes of our story, we have thought it possible that he perhaps met them in his youth, even during what may have been Jesus' first Feast of the Passover.

Our reason for inserting these friends into this fictional story is in no way an attempt to re-write the life and history of our Lord and Savior, Jesus Christ. Nor is it to represent words and thoughts coming from the Savior's lips as authoritative and accurate. Rather, it is simply an exploration of how the Savior's increased understanding of his divine mission may have been triggered by his interactions with the friends of his youth.

Our goal, then, has been to create a fictional canvas upon which we can provide possibilities of *color* and *detail* into the Savior's formative years. Elder Neal A. Maxwell, in his book *Look Back at Sodom, A Timely Account From Imaginary Sodom Scrolls* (Deseret Book, 1975), also took this approach, exploring the Biblically historical moment of Sodom and Gomorrah. On the frontispiece of his book, he states: "SUPPOSE someone had kept his impressions of Sodom on several scrolls, which were later found. They might well contain such things as are on the pages to follow." Likewise, we have supposed that perhaps friends of Jesus might have recorded their thoughts and experiences, thus allowing us to look through a magnifying glass at the formative years of his mortal life, as extracted from an imaginary document.

Additionally, we have taken liberties in identifying the early age at which Jesus had full understanding of his divine nature and mission. We have done this for the express purpose of stimulating the reader to consider this undocumented process of *being* and *becoming* as experienced by the Savior. We hope you, the reader, will enjoy this "what if" scenario. We likewise hope that it will give us the opportunity to consider together, not only the Savior's early *righteous* footsteps, but also the positioning of our own feet as we move forward along the Savior's "straight and narrow path."

Part One

THE STUDENT

HEBREW UNIVERSITY

Jerusalem, Israel
September 13, 1994

Shifting my feet nervously, I rolled my favorite mechanical pencil between the thumb and index finger of my right hand while contemplating the unusually good-natured man before me. I especially admired his exceptional prowess as an archeological scholar, a professor of Hebrew, and an instructor of ancient and modern theology. And, I must say, I even liked his long, graying beard. I also liked the fact that, although he was an orthodox Jew, he wore European-style clothing.

Professor Eli Cohen had been speaking for an hour—in perfect English, I might add—on the subject of the sacred Jewish Torah. And, though I was fascinated with the ongoing discussion, I was anxious for the class to end so that the professor and I could drive to the old part of the city, as he had promised.

Old Jerusalem! That's what he'd alluded to earlier in the week, when he had mentioned something about an unknown archeological site and what he kept referring to as "the *find* of a lifetime." For the life of me, I couldn't figure it. Why, indeed, would Rabbi Cohen choose *me* to be a part of some ancient "dig?" And the artifact—*was* it an artifact? And had any others already seen the treasure?

So many questions.

I figured, however, that I'd have the answers soon enough. So, for the moment I sat quietly, with patient anticipation. I couldn't believe it, really. The adrenaline in my body was enough to fuel a spaceship. I'd wanted to be a part of an extraordinary archeological "find" for as long as I could remember. And now, here it was, staring me—Jason Ellis—squarely in the face.

My thoughts left the classroom, the university, and the Holy Land, and I thought of my wife's funeral two years earlier. The pain and anger of her death came again into my heart, and as though it were yesterday, the words of my father echoed in my mind. "Jason," he had said quietly, "you have much to do with your life. You must not allow her death to canker your soul. Instead, have faith in the resurrection and live worthy to once again be with her."

Could this be my "journey of destiny," I wondered? If so, could I fulfill the rabbi's expectations while feelings of anger still loomed so heavy in my heart? My soul had indeed become cankered, almost without my realizing what was happening.

And now, though it had been over two years, my anger against God had only seemed to be uncontrollably growing. It just wasn't fair that a beautiful, compassionate, vibrant woman with her whole life ahead of her could suddenly be taken, without warning. An aneurysm, the doctors had said; there had only been that brief second of pain, and then—nothing. And then I was alone, without her. For the last two years I had been haunted with the question: How could God allow such an unjustified tragedy to rip out the wellspring of happiness that a hopeful young husband had known?!

"The sacred Torah," Rabbi Cohen suddenly shouted, as if to awaken me from my torment, "begins by introducing God, or *Elohim*, as we say in Hebrew, as the accepted creator of the universe. After placing all things in order during six separate time periods, he rested on the seventh. This day, which in Hebrew we refer to as *Shabbat*, means 'he rested,' and is a sanctified day that is still considered holy.

"The essence of our Jewish faith is really quite simple," he continued, obviously getting more wound up as he spoke. "It is found in the book of Leviticus, the third book in the sacred Torah. Those of you who follow Jesus know, of course, that he quoted the writings of Moses on a regular basis. In chapter 19 of this book, it is written, '*You shall love your neighbor as yourself.*'

"My friend, Jason," he continued, smiling directly at me, "has taken this charge very seriously, as he has 'fallen in love' with my two children—Rebecca, who is thirteen, and my Joseph, who is fifteen. He has also fallen in love with my Sarah's cooking!"

The class laughed, as they knew the good rabbi and his family had more or less "adopted" me over the past two years. Although I was appreciative of the rabbi's sentiments, I found my face suddenly red with embarrassment. Why, I wondered, did I always react in this way? My response was no different, and no less visible, than it had been years earlier, when I had been singled out in front of my grade school classmates, whether it had been for a perfect spelling test or for gazing out the window daydreaming. Kirsten, my wife, had loved to tease me because I flushed so easily. My tendency to blush was the one undesirable trait I had inherited from my father, and I was beginning to think that I never would grow out of it.

"Now, class," Professor Cohen continued, oblivious to my discomfort, "you should likewise know that Muhammad, the founder of the religion of Islam six centuries after Jesus was born, also had great respect for the ancient prophets. He revered Moses as a true prophet of God, and called us, his Jewish cousins, 'the people of the Book.' The main commandment, the very central notion of his teaching, was that man must profess that *Allah*, or God, is the only true God."

As I shifted positions in my uncushioned seat near the back of the room, I was mesmerized by the soothing sounds of Professor Cohen's voice, his forever-wise facial expressions, and his professional stature. He was a dynamic speaker, a trustworthy advocate, and a truly wonderful friend. In fact, I'm quite certain that had it not been for his timely intervention two years back, when I'd gotten myself into trouble by sneaking into an ancient tomb complex, I wouldn't be here today.

There are just some places in Jerusalem that you don't invite yourself into.

I still believe the locals who caught me would have really worked me over, if it hadn't been for the professor. And, of course, since I did come here to Hebrew University to study, I should have been more respectful in my explorations.

In any event, there is one thing for certain. Without the professor on my side, I would have been dismissed from my doctoral program and shipped back to the States in my first semester of studies.

So, from the very beginning, the old professor and I hit it off just right. I suppose he knew that I wasn't just some wealthy American's son, eager for a semester abroad. No way! I had earned my way through undergraduate school, and he knew it. He also knew I had received a fellowship to assist me financially, and he respected me for that, as well. He knew the commitment it took to leave one's culture, enter a three-year doctoral program, and pay the price for that depth of education.

As he concluded his lecture, I thought of the way he had about him. I felt like he could pierce a concrete wall with his penetrating gaze. Two years earlier, when he had looked into my eyes for the first time, I saw something that I don't believe anyone else in the classroom saw—

A *light*! That's right, a light. I saw the rabbi's eyes illuminate like a set of crystals glimmering in the noonday sun. It was the single most remarkable phenomenon I have ever witnessed. And, although I have questioned the actual occurrence of the event more than once, in the back of my mind I am certain of what I saw on that day, and simply have no logical explanation it.

In truth, he had the kind of look in his eyes that brilliant thinkers get when they're suddenly delighted at some new discovery they've made, or when an unexpected answer they've been seeking hits them in the head like a sledgehammer. They suddenly know which direction to take in their endeavor, whatever it may be. Anyway, that was the look I saw in the professor's eyes on the very first day of my initial semester at Hebrew University.

The whole experience had been strange, really. The rabbi had posed a rather personal question that morning—"Why are *you* here?"—then had gone from student to student, seeking a response from each one, looking directly into their eyes. When he came to me, he hesitated for a second or so, then said, "Why are you here, Mr. Ellis?"

"Sir?" I asked, unsure precisely what he wanted.

"It's Jason, right?" He began scanning my heart, down through what I felt was a conduit at the back of my eyes. I could feel it!

"Yes, sir," I answered.

"And, who is this Kevin Costner fellow you are supposed to resemble? This *is* the person your friend, Melissa, likened you to . . . is it not?"

Glancing awkwardly over to my new friend and classmate, Melissa Jones, I found myself blushing. She had made the reference only moments earlier, as the two of us had entered the classroom together.

"Uh . . . he's an American film star, sir." Just making the comparison out loud sounded phony to me, and uncharacteristically arrogant. People had been making the comparison ever since his movie *Dances with Wolves*, and although I was inwardly complimented by it, still the public reference embarrassed me.

"I'm afraid I'm not one to indulge in movie-going," he continued, "so forgive me for not making this connection myself."

Again the class laughed, enjoying the jovial nature of the middle-aged Jewish professor, and mutually appreciative that his joking was not at *their* expense.

"So, tell me, Jason," he added, suddenly getting serious, "are you really interested in studying Hebraic dialects, or merely intrigued by the fascination and hope of discovering a language of such ancient origin?"

"Well, sir," I replied, relieved that he had dropped the subject of my looks, "I have a deep love for Semitic languages, especially Hebrew and Arabic, which are still spoken today. In fact, I've been dreaming of doing my doctoral studies here in the Holy Land for as long as I can remember."

"You don't say. . . ."

"Yes, sir," I reaffirmed, "I *do* say!"

Professor Cohen focused his gaze directly into my eyes, and like a sophisticated television camera lens, the iris in his eyes opened and closed slightly, without his taking his eyes away from mine. Then he added, "And, Mr. Ellis, would you care to tell the class how you've financed your studies here—in addition to your fellowship, of course."

Shifting uncomfortably, yet wanting to answer honestly, I replied, "Well, sir, I worked construction this past year, after completing my masters program; and my parents are assisting me, as well. I have a passion for Middle Eastern languages, sir, and right now my doctoral studies mean everything to me."

"Then you're a serious student, Mr. Ellis."

His statement seemed to be just that, and not a question, and so I answered, "Most definitely, sir."

"That's good, Jason. It is exactly what I hoped you would say."

Then, for an instant, before he turned away from me and toward my roommate, Sid Pershings, his eyes suddenly lit up, and for the life of me I swear I saw a faint, yet undeniable flash of white light surging outward from deep inside his soul! Then something else happened that set my heart on fire. At that instant, I heard a barely audible whisper as he said, "*You* are the one. . . ."

From that moment until this very day, I have felt a bond with Professor Cohen that is unlike anything I've ever experienced. I liked him immediately; and now, after two years of taking classes from him and interacting with his family in their home, I have gained an admiration and respect for the man that is equal to none. In fact, when he asked me if I would be interested in viewing a Christian-era artifact that he said had been seen by only one other person, I was simply overwhelmed. It was what I'd waited for all my life.

"What?" I had asked. "Are you kidding, Professor?"

"Kidding?"

"It's just an expression, sir," I went on, feeling the excitement of the moment. "It just means that, yes, I would *love* to see the artifact!"

He spoke briefly about the "find," without ever describing anything in detail, then told me that for the time being we shouldn't discuss the matter further, but that it had to be kept strictly confidential. Apparently the professor had possession of the artifact and wanted to keep it that way. So I said nothing further about it, except to accept his generous offer of a personal viewing.

Now, in quiet desperation, I found myself wanting, *willing* the final few minutes of the class to pass more rapidly. I looked around the room at several of my classmates, then refocused my attention toward the front. The rabbi was concluding his lecture; and although

I tried to transform his words into meaningful notes, it was a useless endeavor. I was hopelessly paralyzed by the incessant daydreaming going on inside my head—and over-energized by the anticipated excitement of the hours awaiting.

At exactly 3:55, a full five minutes before the class was to be dismissed, Rabbi Cohen ended his lecture abruptly, sending everyone home.

"Jason?" he said quietly, as I too began making my way toward the front exit. "Where are you going?"

I looked about the room, and noted that both Sid and Melissa had left. "I thought I'd wait outside in the hallway," I answered.

"Nonsense," he countered. "Did you forget about our little excursion this afternoon?"

"No, sir," I responded politely, "not at all. In fact, I just figured that you wanted to keep it quiet, and, well, I was going to wait. . . ."

"Come here, my friend," he directed, effectively cutting me off in mid-sentence. "Sit in that seat over there by the window." He raised his right hand and pointed with a gnarled finger toward the desk nearest his podium. Lowering his voice he then continued. "None of the other students have the slightest idea why I have asked you to remain behind, Jason. And, since there are a few things we should discuss before our short journey, please sit with me and let me share some of my thoughts with you."

"All right." *All right? Is that the only thing I could think of to say?*

Obediently, I walked over to a small desk by the window, sat down as instructed, then gave my complete attention to the old professor.

"Have you been thinking about our conversation last week, Jason?" he probed.

"Yes, sir," I answered, " . . . every day, in fact."

"And you are certain that you want to proceed?"

"Of course, sir."

"Yet, you know nothing about the artifact?"

"Nothing," I replied. "You didn't say much about the object, except that you wanted its existence kept quiet. Am I right?"

"You are right, Jason. And you haven't said a thing, even to your parents?"

"No, not even to my parents," I confirmed solidly. "You never gave me so much as a clue as to what it is you intend to show me, and for that reason, among others, I haven't spoken of it to a soul. Besides, what would I tell him, anyway?"

The rabbi said nothing. He just sat there and stared directly into my eyes.

"I've *kept* my silence, Professor," I blurted out, feeling uncomfortably defensive by the unexpected silence. "I've told no one!"

For a moment longer the old rabbi held his gaze and said nothing. Yet, as he continued to probe my eyes with his own, I felt as though he didn't believe me, and was trying to extract the truth by searching my soul through my eyes. Still, I knew I had been true to his wishes, and somehow he would know that—if, in fact, he was able to look into my heart.

"This is your last year in our program, yes?" he inquired suddenly. And, although he had known me throughout my entire two years of study, I said simply, "Yes, sir."

"One of the other professors informed me that you have already began your dissertation . . . your prospectus, I mean. . . ."

"Yes, sir," I began nervously. "In deference to your busy schedule, I have asked Rabbi Goldman to serve as my doctoral chairman. He accepted, of course, and now I have defined my study, dealing with Hebrew etymology, and—"

"Never mind all that," he interjected sharply. "I have spoken with Rabbi Goldman, and have replaced him as the chairman of your dissertation committee. You will 'change course,' as you Americans say, and begin all over again."

"Begin all over again?!" I protested, thinking about the many hours I had put into the project with Rabbi Goldman. "What do you mean, sir?"

"I mean that you must discard your study on Hebrew etymology," he replied.

Then, without speaking further, he turned, picked up his old wooden cane—a crutch that had become his trademark—and beckoned me to follow. Stumbling to my feet, I gathered my books into my arms and followed him out the door.

A few moments later, after being picked up at the university by the rabbi's friend, Jacob, I found myself riding in a dilapidated taxi cab as we circled the old city toward the entrance known as Jaffa Gate.

"Jason," Rabbi Cohen began, at last breaking his silence, "tell us, if you would, what you understand about the famous Dead Sea Scrolls."

"I beg your pardon, sir?"

"Just . . . how do you say . . . spit it out. My friend Jacob and I are an appreciative audience."

"Well, Rabbi, to be honest, I know very little. I do know that the scrolls were found just a few miles west of here, on the northwestern shore of the Dead Sea."

"Do you know *when*, Jason, and by *whom?*"

"I have heard, sir, but I honestly don't remember. I've been to the site, of course, but that was two years ago. And, since I have just begun to study the scrolls in depth, in preparation for my dissertation, I really can't answer you."

"No matter, Jason, no matter at all. My friend, Jacob, knows much of it, but usually leaves the explaining to me. So, if you're interested, I'll give you a brief synopsis of what have been heralded as the most exciting ancient scrolls ever to be found."

"Thank you, sir," I coughed, my response feeling entirely inadequate.

"Very well. Late in the year 1946, as you may recall, several young boys of the *Ta'amireh* tribe of bedouin were exploring the six caves in the area of *Khirbet Qumran,* which translated means the ruins of the house of Qumran. They were displaying their strength by throwing rocks into one of the caves, and were surprised to hear the sound of pottery breaking below. They mustered up their bravery, then entered this cave, now known as Cave One. As they suspected, they found the rubble of broken jars and other debris on the floor of the cave. A few jars were still intact, however, so one of the boys opened these and found three ancient parchment scrolls inside."

"The boys were surely led there by Jehovah," the man Jacob interjected with a thick, husky Hebrew accent. His words were the first he had uttered since I had gotten into his antiquated automobile, and came as quite a surprise to me.

"Most assuredly, Jacob," Rabbi Cohen continued. "The contents, Jason, were astounding, as they were Hebrew writings dating back to the first century B.C. In fact, the largest of these scrolls was a complete Book of Isaiah—the oldest ever discovered!"

"That I remember," I whispered, details of the "find" now coming back to me.

"Well, my young American scholar," Rabbi Cohen added, "it will be the study of a lifetime for you to learn what there is to know about this truly inspired discovery. But, to be brief, four other scrolls were later found in the ruins on the cave floor. Even later still, literally thousands of fragments of additional parchment manuscripts were taken from the other five caves in the area, then sold by the bedouin to interested parties.

"It was over a year," he continued, "before these scrolls found their way into the hands of my predecessors here in Jerusalem. An Israeli professor, E. Sukenik, of our university, was asked to initially appraise one of the parchments. He immediately announced that he was looking at a genuine manuscript from the Second Temple period. He is now deceased, of course, but at that time his words brought much notoriety to our land.

"I'm sure you have learned, Jason, that Professor Sukenik and his associates were elated with the discovery, and by the spring of 1948 had permitted the news of this grand literary treasure to be released to the outside world. Imagine—ancient scrolls, including the oldest Biblical manuscripts ever found, discovered within an hour's drive from where we are now."

"May I ask you a question, Rabbi?"

"Certainly, Jason. Please, do ask."

"Was Jesus of Nazareth even *mentioned* in these scrolls?"

"To my knowledge, no," Rabbi Cohen replied, obviously knowing where my Christian mind was leading me. "But, remember, these writings were mostly completed prior to your Jesus of Nazareth living in this region. Some are dated as late as 68 A.D., however, although no mention is made of him."

"Were these people Jewish?" I pressed, my interest piqued by what I was being told.

"Yes . . . most certainly. The people who occupied the area were a Jewish sect known as the *Essenes*. They were a highly religious society, of course, and much evidence has since been unearthed that showed them to be a very prayerful and devout sect.

"You may have learned," the rabbi continued, "that my predecessors eventually unearthed an entire community, including building remains, tables and benches upon which to sit and write, as well as hoards of silver coins. The coins were likewise stored in earthen jars."

"What became of this people?" I then asked, feeling a sense of increasing clarity with what I was now learning.

"Well, my friend," the rabbi answered, "they actually deserted the area twice—the first time after a fire and earthquake came upon them, around 31 B.C. The buildings and water system then remained unused until they were rebuilt around 4 B.C. The Essenes then flourished until they were conquered by the Romans during the Jewish war against them, between 67 and 74 A.D. At the end, a small group of these persecuted Essenes fled several miles to the south, to the ill-fated Masada. As you know, Jason, thousands of Jews and Christians were killed by the Romans during those wars. Of course, the religious zeal, both of the Jews and your Christ followers, created this animosity. But then, I suppose the growing belief in your Jesus' resurrection was the basic justification for this mass destruction."

"I suppose so," I answered, recalling in my mind the "darkness" I had felt when visiting the Masada site—also during my first semester at the university.

Rabbi Cohen was suddenly quiet, gazing out the window at the small herd of sheep that grazed to our right. My thoughts were focused now, wondering how a Jewish scholar could so easily pass over the significance of Christ's existence, not to mention the global written testimonies regarding his literal resurrection. I respected the Jewish rabbi, to be sure, but *why* could he not see that the promised Messiah had, indeed, come to the earth, and had identified himself as none other than Jesus of Nazareth—the literal Son of God?!

"Well, Jacob, this is where we must part," Professor Cohen suddenly announced.

The car came to a stop, and after a brief but cordial parting, I accompanied this unusual Jewish rabbi as we passed through what was known as Jaffa Gate. From his shoulder hung a large, obviously hand-made cloth bag. It seemed unwieldy for him to carry, and I thought it intriguing that he would carry such a cumbersome burden on this mysterious trek. Perhaps the bag contained the tools we would need when we arrived at his "undiscovered" dig.

Thinking no more about the bag, we walked slowly past what the rabbi explained was David's Citadel, then south, down through what I had learned was the Armenian Quarter of the ancient city.

Suddenly stopping, Professor Cohen put out his free arm, halting my footsteps.

"Before continuing, Jason, let me tell you of that gate over there to our right."

As the rabbi pointed into the mid-afternoon sun, I saw what appeared to be the ruins of an ancient city wall. "That is where the old Essene Gate once was," the rabbi continued. "I spoke of the Essenes earlier, in describing the authors of the Dead Sea Scrolls. Members of this ancient sect were ultra orthodox—more strict than even the Sadducees. They wouldn't defile the Holy City by relieving themselves within the city walls. Consequently they would go out that gate, use whatever bathroom facilities they had on the hillside, then return to their homes through the same gate."

"Amazing," I muttered, not knowing how else to respond.

"Now, Jason," he continued, gesturing to our left, "let me introduce you to a very special synagogue. Before we go inside, however," he said, pointing to some stones in the foundation, "let me say that the structure that stands here now was built in the exact location of the home of a man named John Mark. According to your Christian tradition," he added, obviously enjoying himself and the knowledge he had of Christian history as he continued to emphasize the word *your,* "it was into this home that Jesus took his apostles, and in the upper room shared with them what has become known as the 'Last Supper.' As you no doubt know, it was this John Mark who later become Peter's scribe, and who recorded the second book in your New Testament.

"Just before the Roman destruction of Jerusalem in 70 A.D., a group of Christians fled to Pella, a city on the eastern side of the

Dead Sea—in the modern day country of Jordan. John Mark's home, or the 'Upper Room' building, was destroyed during this Roman invasion. When this group of Christians returned to Jerusalem, they rebuilt the structure into a Christian synagogue.

"Now," he concluded, "let us go inside. . . ."

As we entered the obviously vacant structure, I noticed that his *kippah*, or cap, remained on his head, as it is the Jewish custom of covering one's head when entering a holy place. I knew that, to the rabbi, this tradition was one of respect—a sign of true humility before God. And so, adjusting my baseball cap on my head, I followed him into the synagogue.

"Notice, as we enter, the large, rounded concave indentation in the wall. It is called an *apse,* and is where the Torah would be kept. It always faces north. The Torah apse always faces the temple mount, for it has always been the focal point of the Jewish religion. I, along with a few Christian acquaintances, believe that this change indicates a new focus for the Jewish worshipers who built it; namely, the hill of Calvary and tomb area to the north! Thus, the same 'Upper Room' building appropriately became the new place of worship for the followers of your Jesus and his apostles."

Without reply, I nodded, understanding, then followed the rabbi up the stairway and into a large room on the upper level.

"Here you have it," he smiled, fanning his outstretched arm in a clockwise direction. "The place of your Last Supper."

At this instant, just as I had during my previous visits to the room, I felt totally subdued. Again I experienced a sense of reverence that was impossible to describe. Here I was, standing in the re-built room where Jesus ate with his apostles, washed their feet, and announced his betrayal by Judas Iscariot.

"It must have been a remarkable event," I finally said. "Thank you, Rabbi, for being so considerate as to bring me here."

Motioning toward the only two chairs in the corner, Rabbi Cohen invited me to sit down.

"My wife tells me that I'm a man of surprises," he smiled, sitting down and positioning his large cloth bag in his lap. "And now I must provide you with a gift . . . a very special gift. Before I do, however, let me tell you a story of my youth.

"My father," he continued, closing his eyes as he spoke, "found something of incredible value in the foundation of this very synagogue—over fifty years ago. He kept it to himself, then passed it on to me before his death, just months later. There was an urgent need for secrecy back then, and there remains a need even today—to keep what I am about to tell you a secret from the rest of the world."

To say that I was speechless would be an understatement. Never before had my mind raced so wildly. I somehow knew that something extraordinary was about to take place, and that my life would never be the same because of it.

"I was born in the year 1934, Jason, not more than a mile from where we now sit. In the spring of 1946, when I was but twelve years of age, my father brought me to this very spot—as I said, just weeks before his passing."

By now my mouth was cotton dry, and I found it very difficult to even breathe. I blinked my eyes, and he continued.

"Our being here was extraordinary, Jason, simply because we had no reason to be standing in the upper room of a Christian memorial. However, he explained to me that because his 'find' was of Christian origin, placing it in my care here, above the ancient synagogue, was only appropriate. It was a large oblong vase, which contained three ancient scrolls. He said he had located the vase while digging for artifacts. He had found it in a cave-like hole a full two feet below the earthen surface of this very structure."

Allowing his words to sink into my mind, Rabbi Cohen smiled broadly, then opened the bag before him. Placing both of his hands inside, he extracted what looked to be an ancient, oblong container.

"There they are," he exclaimed, unable to contain his excitement, "the very scrolls he discovered over 50 years ago!"

"But, Rabbi," I questioned, "I don't understand . . . I. . . ."

"But, let me continue, my son. We may be interrupted, and I want to conclude my story."

Seeing that he had made his point, Rabbi Eli Cohen allowed this unusual experience to unfold.

"My friend," he stated, now whispering urgently, "what I am about to tell you must be kept in the strictest of confidence. I knew from the moment I first saw you that you were the *one* I had been waiting for."

"Waiting for?" I pressed, trying desperately to understand. "I'm not sure I follow you, Professor. . . ."

"You see," he pressed, gazing directly into my eyes, "my father swore me to secrecy, then instructed me that because of his suddenly failing health, his productive translating days were fast escaping him. He then told me that when the time was right, I should begin translating the first set of scrolls. He said that my translating the first few parchments would give credibility to the find; but that I should then pass them on to someone trustworthy enough to accept them for what they are—and to thus allow that person to complete the translation of not only this first set of scrolls, but the other two sets, as well. Father himself had been tutored in the translation process by the same Professor Sukenik who, only weeks later, was given the Dead Sea Scrolls to translate.

"And so," he concluded, "in one quiet meeting, my father gave me to know that I would also become a translator of the ancient scribal languages, even as he had been, and that I would be entrusted with parchments of unparalleled value. *These* scrolls," he coughed, lightly tapping the ancient parchments in his lap, "were written in Hebrew, as were the Dead Sea Scrolls—"

"But," I stammered, at last interrupting the rabbi, "why was he so secretive?"

"Don't you get it, Jason?"

"Get what, sir?"

"He *couldn't* tell anyone locally about the find, or it would have ruined his rabbinical career, and his much-needed reputation."

"What are you talking about, Professor?"

"The scrolls, Jason! The Magdalene Scrolls! They were *Christian* scrolls! The Jewish people don't believe that Jesus Christ was anyone more than a teacher! His words discounted, even mocked, many Jewish beliefs! Can't you understand that? If my father had shown his find to the world, it would have brought great shame to our people, because we're the ones . . . who . . . *crucified him!*"

"Thank you, Professor. I . . . I think I'm beginning to understand. You used the term, *Magdalene* in referring to the scrolls?"

"Yes. To Father's surprise, he found that this first scroll was written by a woman . . . a very unlikely discovery, considering the fact that few women of that day had the opportunity of learning to write the Hebrew language.

"The woman who authored the first set of scrolls," he concluded, drawing in a deep breath, "which, by the way, are the only scrolls Father and I looked at, was positively identified by father as *Mary of Magdala.*"

"Mary Magdalene?! Christ's friend who was first at his tomb the morning of his resurrection?!"

"Well, yes . . . although of course you know that I do not believe in . . . his *resurrection. . . .*"

"Of course," I agreed, hoping I had not offended him with my statement. "But, Rabbi, how could this—?"

"According to the scroll, this Mary, from the northern village of Magdala, entrusted her story to one she referred to as Mark . . . perhaps the same John Mark who owned this very home in which we now sit. As my father began to translate, he could see that upon these scrolls was a story told by this Mary Magdalene of Galilee. Her identity is revealed on the first parchment, as you will see."

I was again stunned speechless! What was happening? Could this all be a dream, or could I actually be in this sacred building receiving this 2,000-year-old tale from Mary Magdalene?

"Jason, you have a gift with the Hebrew language, and your doctoral studies have fared you well. But you now have a charge that you cannot cast off. Without speaking of this record, you must now do that which I promised my father I would have you do . . . that of being the instrument through which this ancient story comes to life. While I am not a follower of your Christ, I believe in history and know that he lived and died here in Jerusalem. Unlike most orthodox Jews, I appreciate the value of his contribution to mankind, especially his ability to teach and to lift others.

"If you agree to this task," he added, "it will now become the backdrop for your doctoral dissertation . . . and then your own place in history. When you have finished, you will know how, and in what way, you are to reveal the origin of the scrolls. I do not expect you to lie, but to tell the truth . . . *with* the right timing. Premature disclosure could bring disgrace and criticism to my family, that I may not be able to endure."

"Rabbi, I . . . I'm not really sure how to respond; but yes, of course I will translate the sets of scrolls, even though I can't comprehend such a task!"

"That is the remarkable power of it, Jason," he replied, at the same time retrieving the three sets of scrolls, placing them back into their container, then into his carrying bag. "I have lived with this mystery for almost five decades now, wondering how and when the hour for further translation would arrive. Now, as you give your approval, I feel almost as if the weight of the world has been removed from my shoulders. For you see, my young Hebrew scholar, *no one* knows of this artifact—except, of course, my dear companion, Sarah. I have been true to my father's request, and even though he died shortly after giving me his charge, I believe he knows of my obedience. I have often felt of his nearness, and strangely believe that he has helped protect these scrolls . . . even from where he now resides."

Not realizing that this conversation would forever change my life, I asked, "Rabbi . . . does this first set of scrolls have a name . . . I mean, does this story have a title to it? A beginning point?"

"But, of course," the Rabbi smiled, winking as he spoke. "Did I not mention? It is quite obviously a story of your Jesus . . . called *The Carpenter's Son*."

Just hearing the words caused my mind to blur, and my eyes suddenly filled with moisture. Could this experience be real? Could *I really* be so blessed as to be invited on such an unlikely journey? *The Carpenter's Son*, I thought silently, *written by none other than Mary Magdalene*—

"Now, my good friend and colleague," Rabbi Cohen concluded, breaking into the silence of my thoughts, "we must be getting along. The final rays of light are fast falling through the window, and we must get you back to your studies. This evening is the beginning of our Sabbath, as you know. But tomorrow, after our services, and if you have the time, I would like for you to come to my home. We can begin by your reading the first chapter of the initial set of scrolls, comparing it with my translation. It will help you get into the flow of the ancient writing style. You will then be prepared to translate the majority of the text. It will be a discovery process for both of us, Jason, as I restricted my reading to the first chapter that I translated.

It is time, Jason . . . it is time."

Without speaking further, the old rabbi retrieved the antiquated vase and placed it back inside the cloth container. He then turned, picked up his old but reliable cane, and slowly went back down the stairs. I followed, having no idea how prophetic his earlier words would become . . . for truly this journey to the location of John Mark's home would utterly set in motion my rendezvous with destiny!

Part Two

THE STORY

THE CARPENTER'S SON

As Written by Mary and Entrusted to Mark

A.D. 67

I

My name is Mary. I am the daughter of Lamech, of Magdala. I have lived upon the land of my inheritance for more than six decades, and have kept a written record of my devotion to, and dealings with, my Lord and Savior, Jesus Christ.

It is, in fact, this devotion to him that has instilled within my heart a need and a desire to write an abridgment of my personal and historical records.

Since the earliest days of my youth, I have learned from my father the crafts of the scribes, and have written in mine own hand the mysteries and wonders of what I have seen with my eyes, heard with my ears, and felt with my heart. And, although I have sought to perfect my skills as a crafter of words and a keeper of records—despite the traditions of my fathers, who do not consider women capable or worthy of the tasks of the scribes—I have not the talents to adequately describe how I feel in my heart for what I *know* about my Lord. Nevertheless, I will attempt, as I write these pages, to paint a picture, or sketch a silhouette, that might portray the images engraved upon my mind.

Perhaps with a little assistance from the powers on high, those to whom these records will be entrusted will be able to see—from my eyes—who he was, why he was here, and what has become of him since that dark and dreadful morning. It was then that the chief priests, the Pharisees, and the cruel-hearted Romans crucified him on their accursed cross.

Jesus was my friend. I met him early in life, and discovered a remarkable bond of love and adoration for him. He was genuinely kind, and he became an inspiration for good that took such a firm hold on my heart that from that day to this I have devoted my entire talents and energies to his mortal ministry. And, although he was ultimately crucified and taken from this earth, I, Mary of Magdala, do solemnly testify that he is *not* dead, but *lives!* Yes, he lives! He was risen from the grave. He has walked free from that earthen tomb that hid his mortal remains from the rest of the world, and was not constrained to remain here with his enemies. He has regained control of his flesh and bone, and has—through the magnificent powers of his holy priesthood—reunited his body with the eternal soul that was his since the dawn of time.

Jesus is the Lord. He is my God.

How deeply gratified I feel to have been able to walk in his footsteps through the years. How magnificent were those quiet moments of solitude when my Lord walked alone with me, counseled with me, and imparted his wisdom to me. For so often, even though I craved his companionship, I was but one single individual among the multitudes of followers who seemed to tarry relentlessly alongside the Master. Through the years his miracles were many, and his devotion and kindness was continuous. Still, the single most profound moment for me occurred on the morning of the third day following his death.

You see . . . I saw him! I saw him as the resurrected Lord of the universe!

And, oh yes, he did show himself to me in the garden on that day. And I beheld the wounds in his hands and feet—the very places they had driven nails into his flesh before hanging him on the cross three days earlier!

Nevertheless, so great was my joy on the day of his resurrection that even now I am moved to tears. Thus I am constrained to record only the event, rather than the innate feelings of serenity and peace that overwhelmed me; for clearly I cannot find the words to do so.

I *will* say, however, that at first I supposed him to be the gardener, and knew not that it was he. But then he spoke quietly to my soul, and told me to weep not, for he had overcome death, as foretold by so many of the ancients.

But that is the end of his mortal experience. Let me proceed at once with an account of his birth, and the early years of his childhood. I learned of this years later from Mary, the mother of Jesus.

Mary described her first days as a mother as "wondrous times."

"The child was born," she told me, "in a manger, in Bethlehem." For on that day, no rooms were available at the inn, and the tiny prince would not wait.

The elderly innkeeper and his wife had seen Mary, heavy with child, and went out of their way to accommodate the weary travelers. This they did by setting up a comfortable place of solitude in their stables. It was not what Mary or Joseph desired, but was all they had on that night.

As they made themselves as comfortable as possible, a new star appeared in the heavens above them. People from all points on the globe saw it and marveled at its brilliance. For so it was that until that very night, no such star had graced the heavens.

Angels appeared to some shepherds in nearby fields, and told them that a "king" was born in Bethlehem. Wise men, kings in their own lands, also saw the star, and traveled great distances to show their respect by showering the child Jesus with gifts. To many, in fact, it was given them to know that the long-awaited Messiah of the world had been born.

Although I was not yet born, my parents saw the star as well. Even though they did not understand its profound significance, they have spoken of having an inner warmth that permeated their entire beings. They knew only that something wonderful had transpired, and they took great comfort in pondering those things they had seen in the heavens on that night. Jesus had been born, and from that day forward the world's inhabitants would never be the same.

II

Forty days after my Lord's birth, Mary and Joseph, with their infant son, Jesus, bade a tearful and grateful farewell to Phillip and Shanna, the innkeeper and his wife who had been so helpful during their brief but eventful stay in Bethlehem. They made the six-mile trek from Bethany into Jerusalem, taking with them, in an enclosed container, two doves, which would be sacrificed as part of the approaching ceremony and would provide a blessing of faith on the heads of the little family.

Mary told me of the feeling of awe that came over her as she and Joseph ascended the stairs of what had first been Solomon's temple, built a full thousand years earlier. It had been destroyed twice since that time, but each destruction was followed with a renewed effort to rebuild and re-sanctify.

At the temple, the high priest Simeon awaited them. He had long ago received the promise, through the Holy Ghost, that he would not taste of death until he had looked upon the Lord Jesus in the flesh. At the sight of Joseph and Mary, the old woman Anna, who had long been a worker in the temple, clapped her hands for joy. "It is my Lord and Savior!" she exclaimed. "The Lord, and these my brethren, have given me to know that I would prophesy of your son, and proclaim his holy birth to all who would hear my voice. . . ."

When Anna had finished her words, Joseph and Mary humbly

offered the two doves, as they had not the means to bring one dove and a lamb, as was expected for the full sacrifice. Though they feared the Lord's displeasure, Simeon reassured them that replacing the lamb with a second dove offering was completely acceptable and was, in fact, given more frequently than the lamb.

Looking upon the infant Jesus, Simeon gave thanks to God. "Lord," he began, "now let thy servant depart in peace, according to thy word. For mine eyes have seen thy salvation, which thou hast prepared before the face of all people—a light to lighten the Gentiles, and the glory of thy people Israel."

Under the spirit of prophesy, Simeon told the gathering crowd of the child's mission and of the anguish his mother would be called upon to endure because of him. "It will be," he concluded, looking at Mary, "like unto that of a sword piercing your soul."

Both Mary and Joseph winced as Simeon spoke his words, and Joseph pulled Mary close to him. They had not considered the consequences of their new stewardship, nor could they imagine others rejecting him. While neither spoke, both looked anxiously into each other's eyes and shared the new emotions that stirred within them.

As the ceremony concluded, they accepted the child back and quietly departed the temple grounds. Both were stunned by the unique and unsolicited experience with Simeon and Anna, and discussed the matter between them. They simply did not know what to make of it all. What they did know was that Jesus, their son, had complied with Israelite law and was now the declared and consecrated firstborn of their new family.

––––––––––––

While it has been years since Mary, the mother of my Lord, passed away, her expressions of pride as a new mother still sing praises to my soul. She was always humbled to think that the Father had selected her to not only give birth to the Only Begotten Son, but to rear him in the favor of God. This she did with dignity, lifting her own standard of behavior so that my Lord could move through his childhood undeterred.

I have often thought of my own life and the elevated paths I have walked because of my Lord. From the moment we met, I sensed his unique and edifying spirit. He enjoyed laughing and playing, certainly; but primarily he enjoyed doing, and being, *good*. This "differentness" was intimidating for a time, but as we became better acquainted, his goodly nature caused my own soul to thirst after righteousness. These were feelings I remember from my own childhood.

But to return now to Mary's story and to the events that transpired following Jesus' presentation at the temple.

It wasn't long before Mary and Joseph began to comprehend some of the dangers alluded to by the prophet Simeon. For while spending time in Jerusalem with Joseph's friend, John Mark, word came back to them that Herod, the king of Judea, had issued a proclamation that deeply troubled them. Herod, a truly wicked man, was a descendent of Esau, and so an Edomite. Together with his family, he was despised and hated by the Jews—and with just cause. He had murdered his wife and several of his sons, as well as most of the members of the great national council, the Sanhedrin. He had no regard for human life and detested the Jews as a people.

Herod had invited the inquiring wise men to find the whereabouts of the newborn Christ child, then to return and tell him so that he might likewise "worship" the Lord. This they naively intended to do—until they were warned in a dream not to disclose Jesus' whereabouts to Herod. Upon finding Jesus, they had bestowed their gifts—gold, frankincense and myrrh—then left immediately for their far-away homelands without speaking further to Herod. When Herod learned of this, he swore vengeance, announcing that he would locate, and kill, the new Jewish king.

Immediately following a direct warning of Herod's treachery by the three wise men, Joseph and Mary had yet another visit from an angel.

"*Arise,*" the heavenly messenger stated boldly to Joseph, "*and take the young child and his mother, and flee into Egypt, and be thou there until I bring thee word: for Herod will seek the young child to destroy him.*"

Their voyage to Egypt spared the little family the hellish misery of Herod's massacre of all firstborn Jewish sons. And so, with resolve born of both fear and gratitude for the warning they had received, Mary and Joseph, along with their tiny child from God, passed undetected and unmolested through the villages of Israel. They would be safe for the time being and would remain in Egypt until the Father would direct them to return to Nazareth with the Christ-child.

III

Time passed, and Joseph and Mary, with their two-year-old son, Jesus, finally returned to their home in Nazareth. Herod had died, so his presence was no longer a threat to them. Thus, they felt it was safe to return to the land of their fathers. Life had been difficult for them while in Egypt; but now Joseph was able to resume his carpenter's trade near my own village to the north, and conditions improved.

To Mary, every step Jesus took was important, and every moment she spent with him was precious. She sensed the role she played in his development and quietly went about her tasks as a homemaker, ever watchful of his activities. She bore other children, and her capacity to nurture her family increased.

During these early years of Jesus' life, as he enjoyed many of the common occurrences of childhood, I lived but a few miles to the northwest, in my own village of Magdala. As I look back on that time, I will never forget what feelings stirred within my heart the first time I met Jesus. I was twelve years old, and my family was traveling to the celebrated Feast of the Passover. This feast, a week-long Jewish celebration, was held annually and attended by all who believed in the deliverance of the great Jehovah. I had never before attended the Passover Feast, and I was so excited!

My family, along with perhaps a dozen others, left Magdala early in the morning, walking to the neighboring village of Nazareth, where we would join friends before continuing our journey down into the Jordan Valley.

The sun was still rising when we arrived at the outskirts of Nazareth. Stopping near the front gate of a particular home, Father tethered our donkey, then called out to a man who was just rounding the corner of the dwelling with his own beast.

"Come on, Joseph," he exclaimed, smiling. "We've many leagues to travel before the sun sets in the skies! And, if we wait here another minute, we'll not make it to the plains of Esdraelon before the morrow!"

"Hold onto your walking staff, Ezra," the man Joseph called out, "and show a little patience, will you? We're just about ready to go, but we won't get *two* leagues if we don't secure the necessary supplies."

As my father and his friend, Joseph, spoke, Mary stepped out of the small shop next to their home and tied a securely wrapped bundle of supplies across the back of the beast they intended to take with them on our journey. "Hurry, son," she called back to someone in the shop.

"I'm coming, Mother," a voice came from the shop. It was not a harsh voice, nor a loud one, and when a young boy moved through the door frame into the street, I was surprised at his youth when his voice sounded so much older and wiser than the boys back home in Magdala.

His eyes were kind and his smile sweet as he greeted our family. His eyes seemed to hold mine just a moment, then he turned to help his mother and father finish loading their donkey.

I knew at that moment that he was different from other boys I had met, and although I did not understand his role as his mother did, I knew that his life would be a remarkable one, that he would always speak in that kind, even voice regardless of whatever his life would bring him. I shall always hear in my mind the voice of Jesus. It never failed to pierce my very soul in a way that words cannot express. I knew from the beginning that this boy named Jesus would forever change my life.

As Jesus walked out into the dry, dusty streets beyond, he carried a shepherd's staff as a support during the long journey ahead. I could not take my eyes off him as he looked off into the distance in the direction we would be traveling.

"Hurry, Mother," he called to Mary. "My arm awaits you and shall be here for you to cling to if you are not able to keep up."

"Oh, Jesus," Mary responded warmly, "you must learn patience for others who do not move as quickly as you do."

Joseph smiled when his wife spoke. "Your mother's right, Jesus," he added, smiling at his eldest son. "You're so energetic, so full of life! Everyone who meets you will long to follow you, and yet, how will they keep up with you?" Joseph put a warm arm around Jesus, and I could see the great love between the father and the son, and the great admiration Jesus had for his father, Joseph.

Years later, I would learn from Jesus that of his father's many gifts, Jesus was especially mindful of the way that Joseph attended to the needs and relationships of those around him. For indeed, Joseph of Nazareth was a sensitive, giving man who was loved and revered by all who knew and befriended him. He was a humble and reverent example to his unusual son, day after work-filled day. Jesus later shared with me that he marveled at how his father was referred to as the "Samarital Craftsman" of Nazareth. From what I later learned, the title was well deserved.

"It appears you've brought your family with you," Joseph smiled at me, and I smiled shyly back.

"Just our eldest," father replied. "This is our daughter, Mary, who is attending the feast for her very first time."

"This is indeed a momentous event for you, young Mary," Joseph said warmly. I nodded and dropped my eyes to the ground. I hadn't been able to sleep at all the previous night, although it wasn't proper for a young girl to say so, and yet I somehow thought that Joseph would understand if I had told him.

When my father turned to introduce my mother to Joseph, he found to his surprise that Mary and my mother were already deep in conversation, heads close together. The two men smiled. "Women!" Joseph said, "How do they do it? Friendship seems so easy for them." My father nodded and smiled at me and I smiled back, glad that he was my father.

Joseph called to Jesus to join us. "This is Jesus, our eldest son. He, too, will be attending the feast for the first time, like you," he nodded toward me kindly. "Jesus, this is the daughter of my friend. Her name is Mary." Joseph then smiled at my father and said, "Let us be on our way! The sun is rising rapidly, and soon it will be too hot to travel."

As our fathers walked ahead of us, reminiscing about days gone by, Jesus and I walked quietly side by side. "Uh," Jesus seemed to stammer, "so this is your first feast as well?" I nodded, knowing that the son of my father's friend shared my excitement for the journey.

I realized that it was my turn to speak, but I had no idea of what to say to this young boy. "You have a very beautiful donkey, Jesus," I finally blurted.

As the words escaped my mouth, I knew that I had completely embarrassed myself. Couldn't I have thought of something besides a donkey to talk about? I felt my face begin to burn.

"Yes, we are fortunate to have such healthy, beautiful animals," he said softly.

I was touched by his kindness. The village boys I knew in Magdala would have laughed at me for what I had said. Jesus was different. "So many animals are worn out and abused," I volunteered. "People don't seem to care for their animals."

We walked in silence comfortably after that. Our growing caravan made its way south—out of the hills and into the valley before us. The journey would take two days, possibly three. But with good fortune and mild weather, we would arrive in Jerusalem with ample time to prepare for the feast.

––––––––––––––

I later learned that my Lord's awareness, and his uncanny memory of his pre-earthly activities, were at this young age flooding into his mind at an increasingly accelerated pace. His Father's house, toward which we were bound, was as well *his* house; it had been destroyed twice before and was now under reconstruction for a third time. And, even though it was not dedicated to the sacred ordinance work that made it so special, still his people gathered, finding courage and inner solace in mingling there—especially during the Feast of the Passover.

As we paused to water our animals at the well, I wanted to ask

Jesus how he felt about his first visit to the temple. But I knew what an impossible question that was—I hardly had words to express my excitement myself.

"What do you know of the Feast?" I asked instead.

"Well . . . " Jesus said thoughtfully, "from what Father has told me, and from what I have read in the sacred Torah, it is the feast to celebrate the liberation of the children of Israel from Egyptian bondage, almost fifteen hundred years ago. Of course it is now celebrated along with the Feast of Unleavened Bread, giving us eight days in Jerusalem, instead of just one."

"I didn't know all of that," I answered honestly. Truly, I had never met someone with such understanding. I felt I could ask him the answer to a question I had never understood. "I have never understood how God could send the angel of death to kill Egyptian children. Can you tell me, Jesus?"

"The angel of death?" His face was sober as he looked at me. "Why do you ask?"

I hesitated to tell him my deepest feelings, so I said only, "Father says that you are very wise, Jesus, and that I would do well to learn from you. . . ."

"Then that means he has spoken with my father," Jesus laughed. "And only the heavens know how proud he is of his children. . . ."

Just then a voice sounded from behind us, and from out of the early morning shadows Jesus' mother, Mary, appeared and walked over to where we were talking. "Hurry along, Jesus," she urged affectionately. "Your father has packed the tent, and is ready to place it on Shezra's back." Then, turning to me, she smiled and said, "Good morning, Mary. Did your family rest well last night?"

I would hold my question for another day, I thought. As long as I could remember, the story of the angel of death had haunted me and my father had never been able to explain to me how God could allow the Egyptian children to die. There was something in Jesus' eyes which said perhaps he would have the answer.

"We should have no trouble making the foothills before nightfall," Mary told us. "Besides, if Joseph is correct, the breezes favor us, and it will be a mild day for travel."

Our small caravan, which had now grown to include upwards of one hundred people, departed the campground and wound its way along the path that was worn with centuries of human travel. Through the Plain of Esdraelon we traveled, reaching Ginae at noontime. Then, determining to veer off in the direction of the Jordan Valley instead of taking the hilly route through Samaria, we back-tracked to Scythopolis and finally stopped for the night along the River Jordan, near Salim.

For Jesus, and for myself, it had been a good day. Although the pace had been difficult, still we had been able to visit, and Jesus especially seemed to enjoy learning of my village and of the beautiful Sea of Galilee that bordered it to the west.

The following morning, after doing my chores and eating my morning meal, I went to the well to fill our large water container. Seeing me, Jesus joined me at the well and filled my container for me.

"Good morning, Mary," he said. "Perhaps you found the ground as rocky last night as I did?"

"Indeed I did," I laughed. "In fact, I remember thinking that perhaps I had placed my bedding on top of most of the rocks in the valley. Now, however, I find that I was mistaken."

We laughed together, enjoying a brief moment of camaraderie, before we quickly retreated to the forming caravan. Although I wanted to ask him my question, we knew the urgency with which our fathers were preparing to leave. My question would have to wait.

Before long, our party was on its way, with everyone enjoying the flat and even terrain toward Archelais and Jericho. From what Father had said, I knew that the road up out of Jericho would be steep, and that I must conserve as much energy as possible.

We arrived in Jericho for our noonday meal, and rested briefly beneath the ancient olive trees that grew near the town well before beginning our ascent up out of the deep valley, just north of the Dead Sea. Finally, in the late afternoon, we arrived in Bethany, our final resting point before our last half-hour walk into Jerusalem. I soon learned that it was here we would spend the night, enjoying the hospitality of Joseph's friends, the family of Matthias, of Bethany.

There too I met the three children of Matthias—Mary, Martha, and Lazarus—and soon we were laughing and playing comfortably together. From the beginning I felt like I had found two new sisters in Mary and Martha. I didn't speak as easily as they, but our hearts were "as one," and I knew I had found friends for life. I felt an unexpected kinship with their brother, Lazarus, as well, and felt I had gained another brother.

I was hesitant at first to share my new friend Jesus with these three, and I am ashamed of my selfishness. I had enjoyed his attention for the first days of our journey, and now he was no longer mine alone. As if he sensed my thoughts, however, he took time to reassure me with a smile, a glance, so that I was not jealous when Jesus said quietly to Lazarus when the time had come to part, "What a great spirit is yours, my friend. The day will come when you will open the eyes of many because of the blessings Heavenly Father has in store for you. You will come to know, Lazarus, the magnificent power of the Father, and such knowledge will bring joy to your heart. I am blessed to be your friend, and honored that our paths have crossed."

"Thank you," Lazarus whispered, "but it is I who am blessed to know such a one as you."

IV

Jerusalem!

So much activity! So many new things to see! Homes, shops, merchants and street vendors alike. Men, women, children, and even animals everywhere; bustling about in different directions.

Jerusalem! So immense—so much bigger than I could have imagined. As Lazarus, Jesus, and I entered the gates of the city, the newness was even more compelling than we had expected.

"Tell, me, Mary," Jesus asked as we stopped to water the animals, "can you believe what your eyes see here today?" I looked around at the vastness of the marketplace and the tall buildings that towered above us on all sides.

"Do you mean the buildings?" I asked.

"No, look around you," he said intently. "Tell me what you see."

"Well," I responded slowly, "I don't know. A lot of people, maybe . . . Some tall buildings over there. I'm not sure. I guess it would be easy to get lost."

Jesus turned to Lazarus, who whistled between his teeth. "It's bigger than Bethany, that's for sure."

"Is that all?" Jesus asked. Lazarus and I looked at each other blankly. What did Jesus mean? we wondered.

"Look about you . . . both of you," he insisted, "and tell me what you see. Not the tall buildings or the roads and alleyways, but the people. *The people!* What do you see in their eyes?"

I looked again and saw the wretched display of human suffering and filthiness strewn about on the sidewalks, roads, and public places. It was a scene I hadn't noticed at first, because of the extraordinary masses of ordinary people busily attending to their normal routines. For a moment I just stood there, pained at what I saw. One young woman sat against a wall with three small children, all begging. I saw that the woman was not only poorly dressed but was partially crippled, as well. For there, leaning against a stone wall directly behind the tiny family, was a crude but functional wooden crutch.

"Yes," said Jesus sadly. "A mother . . . crippled and alone with her children, with nothing more to offer than an extended hand and a small hope for the kindness of some passerby. But," he continued softly, almost as if he were talking to himself, "she is not alone. Everywhere there are others just like her, each one seeking the help of a friend or even a stranger."

Together, we scanned the immediate area around us, noting that our parents stood only a few short steps away, as did my new friends Mary and Martha. They were anxiously engaged in their own conversation with a man who was obviously pointing directions.

I turned back to Jesus, who had focused his attention on another child in need. Yet, this time there was evidence of real concern on his face.

"What is it, Jesus?" I asked, looking off in the same direction as my new friend. "What's wrong?"

"That child over there . . ." Jesus said. "I think he's lost his parents."

"Oh, poor thing!" I cried. "We should do something!"

I wanted desperately to run over to my father and get his help. But Lazarus, who had seen the constant, forward progress of the others in our party, suddenly protested. "Come on!" he exclaimed. "We're going to get left behind if we don't catch up!"

But Jesus did not move. Concerned about the lone child's welfare, he desperately scanned the enormous village square in search of either a man or a woman, or both, who might appear to be looking for a lost son.

I was torn between my concern for the innocent boy and my desire to catch up with the others. Still, I did not move until Lazarus pressed the issue again and tugged at my arm.

"Come, Mary!" he said urgently. "We must go! They're leaving us behind!"

Immediately, I felt the fear of losing contact with my parents and decided to hurry after Lazarus. I sensed that the tiny child was in danger, but consoled myself that someone else would feel the same way and offer assistance. After all, I was just a young girl, still dependent on her parents for safety and survival. What good could *I* do for the child, anyway?

As I ran to catch up with my parents, I assumed that my friend Jesus would be behind me. Certainly he, too, had realized the uselessness of trying to lend a hand when the others were waiting for us to follow. And so I hurried after Lazarus until we arrived safely in the comforting shadows of our parents.

Jesus, however, did not hurry after his parents as we had done. Nor was he concerned about the possibility of becoming separated from us. Instead, he began pushing his way through a tangled heap of vendors and shoppers, eventually kneeling down beside the small abandoned child, who was by that time curled up in a fetal position against a stone wall, shivering uncontrollably from fright.

"Little one," he called out gently to the dark-skinned child. "Where are your parents?"

At first the boy said nothing. Clearly terrified at the thought of having been abandoned by his parents and to left face the dangers that seemed imminent around him, he huddled against the wall and sobbed. Jesus reached forward and lifted him up out of the dirt and stench of the street, and the small face lost its fear. Within seconds, a weak but discernible smile spread out unevenly across his lips.

"What's your name, little friend?" Jesus probed, discerning that the child was in need of comfort.

"Simon," the child answered timidly, while wiping a hand across his tearstained face.

"Simon," Jesus said gently. "Why, that's a wonderful name. Is that the name of your father as well?"

"No, my father's name is Simeon." With that, the child realized anew his loss and began to wail, "But now he's gone, and so is my mother. They said they would be right back, but they left me here all alone!"

"They're probably lost, just like you are, and I'm sure they're trying to find you this very moment. This is a big city, Simon, and it's easy for anyone, including grownups, to get lost in the crowds," Jesus said, patting Simon's hand.

"Then how will we find them?" the boy asked anxiously.

"Don't worry about that, little friend . . . we will! I promise!"

Jesus placed the child back down on his feet, then took him by the hand and scanned the area around them, hoping to see one or two adults who might appear to be equally as terrified and anxious about their missing son as he was about them.

"Tell me, Simon," Jesus asked to distract the child from his fears, "you're not from around here, are you?"

"No," the boy whimpered, "we're from Cyrene, in North Africa."

"That's a long way from here," Jesus replied. "But you'll be fine, Simon."

Jesus then withdrew a small piece of cloth from a pocket sewn into the hem of his garment. Carefully, he cleaned the dusty tear stains from the child's face, and continued. "Now, you're going to have to help me. Think very hard, and tell me where you last saw your parents."

"Over there," he pointed, "by the well."

"How long ago?"

"I don't know."

"Well," Jesus encouraged the child yet again, "don't worry about it. We're going to find them, I'm certain of it!"

Gently, then, he led the young boy over to a large fountain at the far end of the plaza. It was here that he planned to begin the search for the lost parents.

"They were right here," the boy cried, a fresh batch of tears cascading down his swollen cheeks. "I saw them talking to that man over there." His little finger trembling as he directed Jesus' attention to a bearded street vendor some distance to the left of where they stood.

As they stood there, Simon told Jesus the story of how his family had traveled many weeks to reach the city of Jerusalem for the Feast of the Passover. "But there were so many people," Simon wept, "and they kept pushing against us until pretty soon I couldn't see Mother and Father." From that moment, he insisted, his only hope had been to pray for a miracle, so that he could find his parents.

"Please don't leave me!" the lad cried.

"I'll stay with you until we find your mother and father, I promise!" And in the child's heart, hope was re-kindled, for clearly the miracle he'd prayed for was taking place.

All this I learned later from Simon. Jesus said little about the episode at that time, although I knew he did not judge me for not staying to assist him. When he did not join us that day, Joseph and Mary, and the rest of us, began to grow fearful. After we had waited several minutes for him, we backtracked to the place where Lazarus and I had last seen Jesus. But neither Jesus, nor the dark-skinned child, were anywhere to be found.

"Where did you last see Jesus?" Joseph questioned intently, holding us out in front of him as he spoke. "And why didn't you insist that he stay with you, rather than wander off like he did?"

"We *did* insist, sir!" Lazarus responded for us both. "But he went to help some little boy and would not listen to us."

"It's all right, children," Joseph comforted us. "It's not your fault. Let's just search here in the plaza and try to find him. He can't have gotten far."

Immediately we turned back toward the open market, then began searching for Jesus.

The search was short-lived, however, as within minutes he was spotted by Lazarus, who saw him delivering the younger child, Simon of Cyrene, to his beleaguered and frantic parents.

Quickly, both Joseph and Mary hurried to where Jesus was conversing with the Cyrenians. Mary and Joseph's concern quickly turned to pride as they saw their son soothing the fears of the child's parents.

"Here is your son," Jesus was saying to the tall man and the emotionally distraught mother. "He was afraid that you had left him behind, and that he might never see you again. But I told him he was mistaken, for I knew in my heart that you *would* come back and search for him for as long as it took to find him. For, so it is with my own parents. I know their love for me is without end, and that they too would search for me, and find me, if I were ever lost."

Simeon, the grateful father of the child, was dumbfounded at the reverent demeanor of the Jewish boy before him, and marveled at the mature calmness of this young boy who had found his son. He extended his burly hand forward toward the unusual benefactor. "How can I thank you?" he asked as he wiped away the tears of gratitude from his eyes.

Ever so gently, and with the unmistakable kindness that was forever manifest in my young Lord's face, Jesus turned to the boy now cuddled safely in his mother's arms. "You are never completely alone," he said to the young boy Simon, "for hope is always alive in the hearts of those who love you. It will see you through difficult times if you will but remember how precious you are in the sight of God."

"Thank you," the boy replied, not altogether certain that he had understood the message delivered by Jesus. Now tired and overwhelmed by the experience, and clearly gratified to be safely reunited with his parents, Simon turned his tiny head into the comforting shadows of his mother's soft and familiar embrace. And, although she too was finding it difficult to speak through her tears, she wanted desperately to reach out to Jesus and tenderly embrace him to show her undying gratitude.

"What is your name?" she asked courteously, wiping away the tears that continued to fall from her cheeks.

"Jesus of Nazareth," the Savior said.

"Dear, young Jesus," she said, "we thank you with all our hearts for what you have done for our son, Simon. What reward can we give you in return for your kindness?"

"I seek no reward," Jesus answered. "Only that Simon should remember this day, and do likewise to another in need when the time is right."

At this the young child looked up and reached out a small, dirty hand. "I will, Jesus, I promise."

Joseph and Mary watched in wonder. They did not intervene in the conversation that was taking place between the Cyrenian family and Jesus, for they were curiously absorbed by the uniquely mature young boy who had been given to them by their Heavenly Father. But Mary, the mother of Jesus, was also grateful for another reason. In her mind, she understood in a way that no other mortal could that her son was also the offspring of the great God of heaven. Surely, his actions and displays of compassion were character traits from on high. Here was a truly magnificent son, who not only understood the powers of mercy and charity, but who increasingly displayed these qualities in his daily life.

Slowly, Mary stepped forward and introduced herself to the Cyrenian family. After hearing of the events that had transpired, she was teary-eyed and emotional as she turned to face her son to listen to what he had to say. Although she felt she should have scolded him for not staying with the main caravan of travelers, she knew in her heart that his charitable acts were his *power* and *purpose* for having come to earth in the first place. He would increasingly act upon his instincts as the Son of God, despite her maternal concern. As if Jesus could read her thoughts, he touched her face gently.

"I'm sorry, Mother," Jesus replied, bringing Mary's thoughts back to the presence. "But this little child could not be left alone."

"You are right, Jesus," Mary replied, inwardly praising his efforts, but outwardly attempting to maintain a stern profile. By doing this she hoped to teach Jesus that, despite his unique position in life, in the future he should at least be more responsible, and perhaps a bit more accountable to his earthly parents.

Joseph seemed equally gratified that Jesus had been found; but like the others around him, he too wished only for Jesus' compliance with the rules of the traveling company.

"Forgive me, Father," Jesus said simply, before he turned away from the family from Cyrene, and followed the rest of us to our sleeping quarters. It had been a long and very full three days since leaving our home in Nazareth; and each of us looked forward to a long and restful night beneath the stars.

I would later learn that on that day Jesus had begun a spiritual quest that would move him quickly into the world of adults, and he felt the weight of this quest squarely on his shoulders. From where I stood, the stars and the heavens had never shined so brightly.

HEBREW UNIVERSITY

Jerusalem, Israel

November 1994

The single lamp in the corner of Rabbi Cohen's living room burned brightly, casting rays of light onto the faces of the good rabbi, his wife, Sarah, and his teenage children, Joseph and Rebecca. They were all seated in a semi-circle in front of me, intently listening as I finished reading my translation of the Simon of Cyrene account.

"This had to have been the same Cyrene," Rabbi Cohen interjected, "who carried the cross of your Jesus on the path to Golgotha."

"Without a doubt," I replied, still in awe over what I had recently translated. The work of the previous weeks of my life had begun in earnest, and now consumed my entire being. I was glad that my course work was completed, so that my time could be spent on this unusual errand. And it was just that, too—an errand. An errand directing two people with entirely different perspectives and agendas. Although my translation was at the unstated request of Mary of Magdala—a devout *believer* in the divinity of Jesus Christ—it had been initiated by a middle-aged Jewish rabbi, Eli Cohen—himself a *non-believer.*

"Jason," the rabbi's wife, Sarah, stated, bringing my mind back to the present, "when you read Mary's words, or at least your interpretation of them, I feel a tenderness in my heart that is unexpected. I am very much *feeling* some of the emotions described by the woman, Mary."

"As am I," the girl Rebecca added. "I am age thirteen, and this Mary, when she first met Jesus, was just a few months younger. I almost feel I have been walking in her shoes."

"I think we're all experiencing unexpected emotions," Rabbi Cohen interjected. "Still, children, we must not mistake emotion for belief. As our fathers before us have taught, we are not looking upon Jesus as anyone more than an intelligent historical figure. We must remember that after all else is said, he was *not* resurrected, he is *not* the promised Messiah, and we must *not* buy into the emotion that he was.

"Jason," the rabbi continued, turning to me, "my family and I know and feel the historical value of what you are doing, and we are prepared to acknowledge our involvement and support at the proper time. However, we must do this as historical custodians. Even so, we must not be swayed by the compelling spirit of the ancient journal-keeper, Mary."

"Thank you, father," the rabbi's son, Joseph, replied. It was the first time he had spoken since we had gathered, and his voice startled me. "Like you and grandfather, I am proud to follow in your steps as a spiritual leader of our people. Accepting the authenticity of this woman's record does not necessarily lead to accepting her Jesus for who he claimed to be."

The conversation continued, and although I had initially rejoiced in being able to share the unfolding story of Christ, more and more I was experiencing frustration. I ached to think that Rabbi Cohen and his endearing family did not *feel* the power of testimony that was so forcefully written on the scrolls. How could they doubt? How could they be so blind as to reject the singular greatness of the twelve-year-old Jesus? It simply didn't make sense.

My only other regret, as I sat in the presence of the Cohen family, was that my wife and two friends, Melissa and Sid, were not sharing this experience with me. I longed for the moment when my lips would no longer be sealed, and when I could explore the ancient scrolls with other *believers* like myself. Still, for the time being I would be patient—both with the denial by the Cohen family and with Rabbi Cohen's "timing" of a public acknowledgement of the scrolls.

And so, as our evening of sharing concluded, and I bid my hosts farewell for the night, my mind continued to sort through the many issues before me. I knew, as I made my way out of the old city and toward my dorm, that for now I must concentrate on the one task of translating. For me, this was a joyous task as well as an escape from the darkness that surrounded me when Kirsten's death tore at my heart. Despite the years that had passed, I could not resolve the feelings of anger and frustration at the loss of her life. It just didn't make sense to me. And so, in spite of my exuberance for my work, peace eluded my grasp.

Jerusalem
A.D. 13

V

The great day of the Feast of the Passover finally arrived. Despite the confusion and disarray in the temple courtyard, the crowds were orderly. My new friend Jesus marveled at the mutual focus and purpose of everyone in attendance. As with each of the rest of us, Jesus participated in everything he could.

As the days passed, Jesus found himself caught up in the endless availability of information and opportunities for learning. Being thus involved, he could not refuse a chance to share some of his own knowledge and insight as he spoke to a group of highly intelligent and astonished priests and doctors. Mary, Martha, and I, and also Lazarus, were seated not far away, marveling at the daily scene as it regularly unfolded.

While Jesus had initially been perceived by these theologians as a common Jewish boy, they soon realized, as did we, that his thoughts and insights reached far beyond his formative years. So profound were his statements, in fact, that by the end of the week, he was not only participating, but was actually leading many of the discussions! In his inspired way of thinking, he reasoned about things that no other living soul could comprehend. Constantly his insightful mind would analyze points of discussion, and he would seize teaching moments to impart of heavenly perspectives that he had, even in this early hour of his mortal life, been given to understand.

Thus it was that at every turn of their conversations, Jesus would prepare simple ways to teach others the concepts of eternal salvation. This he did with a love that was so complete and so unique that he paved the way for men and women alike to understand the greatest commitment of all—the love of God and charity for all humankind.

"Brethren," he taught, "the capacity to love God and to give love is the greatest element of character found inside the human heart. Petty jealousies and prideful thoughts only lead us down a path from which few return."

His words, and their intended message, once again entered the minds and hearts of those listening. Their response, to their own credit, was increasingly one of awe and respect. Who was this man-child, they asked themselves, and how could it be that such a small child could utter such words of wisdom?

Yes, Jesus was still a boy, but within his heart, he had already gained the gentle mannerisms of a God. He was, without doubt, beginning to be perceived as a prince to a "Heavenly Being of Love." It was this capacity to give love, in fact, that later bestowed upon him the humbling title of the world's Prince of Peace.

And so, from that early hour at the temple, Jesus grew in stature and confidence before the great and learned minds of Jerusalem. Tenderly, and without pretense, he was proffering nuggets of truth that surpassed all reasonable expectations.

Thus it was that at the conclusion of the festivities, and on the morning that Joseph and Mary and the rest of our traveling party prepared to leave Jerusalem, Jesus managed to slip away unannounced and return to the temple. While the temple itself was to some extent being reconstructed, still its courtyard served as a meeting place, and it was no different on this day. Consequently, as this group of scholars reassembled, they immediately became immersed in discussing some of the deeper doctrines of the kingdom. And, although Jesus should have followed after his parents, who, with our family, had commenced their long journey homeward, he had felt compelled to remain behind and be about what he later described to his concerned mother, as his "Father's business."

For a full day, meanwhile, we traveled homeward, supposing that Jesus was with our party. However, when Mary and Joseph discovered that Jesus was nowhere to been, they immediately returned to Jerusalem, at last finding their son teaching in the temple.

From what she recorded, Mary was astonished, just as she had been earlier, at what might appear to be an almost blatant lack of discipline. Even so, when she listened anew as her divinely inspired son described his compelling need to do the work he felt was his to do, she realized that it would only be a matter of time before he would go out into the world and begin the process of recruiting human souls for the heavenly armies of God.

"Come, Jesus," she said softly, beginning to cherish every single minute of her time with him. "We simply must return to Nazareth. The others are already arriving at their homes, and are undoubtedly wondering what dangers may have befallen us."

Obedient to his mother's request, Jesus fondly bid his friends farewell. Then, in quiet retrospection, he accompanied his parents down the front steps of the temple and onto the path that led out of the city. He appreciated the gentleness of their rebuke, sensing that it was one of love and concern, rather than of annoyance. For, although they were his custodial parents, he knew that they knew who he was; and that this experience at his first Feast of the Passover would only accelerate his growth into manhood, and then Godhood. More than ever before, he realized that he was on a singular path—not only a path of perfect righteousness, but one of teaching, and of helping others to likewise perfect their own lives.

Jesus would later share with us how he came to know Joseph of Arimathea on the afternoon of the second day of the trip homeward from the feast. When we had left the village of Jericho, Jesus decided to walk ahead of the group. No doubt it was a curious mixture of thoughts that compelled him to do so, for constantly his mind was driven by a spiritual understanding that was his alone as the divine and literal Son of God.

So it was that in the quiet solitude of the morning, Jesus stood by a dry and barren field of freshly plowed earth. Quite suddenly, he noticed an elderly man planting seeds in a garden. Jesus watched for a moment as the old fellow turned the soil over and over again, carefully dropping individual seeds into the earth for a future harvest.

As at so many times earlier in Christ's short-lived sojourn on the earth, he now discovered that his fertile mind seemed to understand the inner core of things. He knew that if he focused his mind, he was able to comprehend the very life-giving pulses of the dormant kernel, thereby understanding the actual makeup of the seed. He marveled at the understanding granted him by the Father regarding not only the yellowish brown seed, but all of the plants and wildlife about him. These discoveries filled Jesus with awe, and reverently he thanked his Heavenly Father for this knowledge.

Momentarily then, while reflecting on the same, Jesus saw something else that fascinated him. It was a unique and truly amazing fact that within the world, hundreds of smaller worlds existed. These were within the framework of the mountains, the oceans, the plants and animals, the trees and the soils, and even the tiny seedlings that were, at that very moment, being planted into the ground by the nameless farmer before him.

He watched the farmer with interest.

"What are you planting there?" he questioned politely, while venturing away from his own thoughts.

The farmer turned with a start, and faced the inquisitive Jesus.

"Who are you?" he questioned.

"I am Jesus," the Savior responded, "the son of Joseph of Nazareth."

"Nazareth?" the farmer questioned, standing upright for a moment and looking straight in the eyes of the youthful Jewish boy. "Well, my young Nazarene friend, if you must know, I am planting an assortment of things."

"Oh?"

"Yes. Several different types of beans and lentils, to name a few. But, why do you ask? Are you the son of a farmer, yourself?"

"No sir," Jesus answered respectfully. "I am a carpenter's son. Still, I've always been fascinated with farming."

"Have you now?"

"Oh, yes sir. Many times, in fact, when my uncle has gone out into the fields to plant his crops, I have worked with him, learning a great deal about the earth and its life-producing powers."

"You sound like a well educated lad, Jesus. But tell me, are you following in the footsteps of your father, or would you rather learn the ways of the farmer?"

"As a matter of fact," Jesus grinned, "I have always fancied the sea and have thought that I would do well as a fisherman."

"A fisherman, eh? That's another noble profession. But tell me, future fisherman, what brings you all the way out here along the road to Nain?"

"I am traveling with my family back from Jerusalem," Jesus said.

"Ah," said the farmer, "your family returns from the great Feast, is that it?"

"Yes, sir," Jesus said with enthusiasm, "the Feast of the Passover. It was my very first time to attend!"

"Well, young Jesus," the farmer went on, "all of us, as you well know, must attend the event once before we become of age. So, what did you make of it?"

While Jesus watched for his mother and father to catch up, he found himself endeared to this new friend and wanted once more to sit and talk for a while. But this time, he understood the urgency of keeping with his family, so quickly shared the events that had been most enjoyable to him during the celebrated occasion.

"Well, sir," he began, again looking over his shoulder, "the entire eight-day celebration was very special for me. I felt a great stirring within my breast as my father killed the lamb for our family and the families we were traveling with. We had to make wooden side-posts on the door of our tent, of course, upon which to place the blood from the lamb. As Father sprinkled this blood on the posts and the lintel, my heart seemed almost to stop. I thought it strange that my spirit felt like I was back in time fifteen hundred years, and that I was watching the angel of death pass over the Israelite homes, then take the life of the firstborn of each Egyptian household. That was a very painful emotion, sir."

The old farmer did not speak. Instead, he simply stared at the youthful Jesus, his eyes brimming with tears invited by the way this mere lad was describing the meaning of the feast. He was likewise impacted by the maturity of words and thoughts expressed by this boy, almost as though he was listening to the wisest of men.

"My father," Jesus continued thoughtfully, "was very particular about serving the roasted lamb. No bone had been broken, of course, and we ate standing, as though we were an Israelite family preparing to hastily leave our captivity by the Egyptians. It was also for this reason that we ate unleavened bread, as there had been no time for the ancient ones to take time for the bread dough to rise. And to represent the bitterness of our people's captivity, we partook of bitter herbs."

Glancing once again over his shoulder, Jesus saw that Joseph and Mary were but a few rods from where he and the farmer stood. So, clearing his throat, he made a final comment.

"I must be going, kind sir; but before I do, may I share my greatest memory of the feast?"

"Please do," the farmer replied, smiling warmly at this unusual and entertaining lad. "I shan't interrupt."

"It was the holy temple, sir . . . the temple and what I learned there. The blood of the sacrificed lamb is an omen of the coming Jehovah, and his sacrifice, sir. It is he who will ultimately deliver God's people . . . as the sins of man are paid for."

"And how is that done, young Jesus? Surely you must know."

"I'm still trying to understand, of course," Jesus mused, "but I am learning more and more, and I think I know the key to having Jehovah's atonement apply to one's own soul."

The farmer was now transfixed, having forgotten that the person speaking to him was but a youth. He found that it was all he could to keep up with the power each word had in his mind.

"Of course we must obey God's laws, building upon the commandments as they were given to Moses, the first deliverer. But there is more to this key, sir, and I think it is found in the first two commandments. If we love Heavenly Father with *all* our heart, then we will not only lose the desire to do evil, but we will then be ready to spend our days turning the *key* of which I speak."

"And that key is . . .?" the man asked, unsure of where the boy's mind was taking him.

"It's simple!" Jesus exclaimed, throwing his arms into the air and then letting his hands slam down on the dust-packed hem of his garment. "We learn to *love!* We *do* love our neighbor as ourself. When we awaken each day, we pray for them and their needs. Then, while we spend our day working, we do all in our power to care for their needs. You see, sir, we become the hands of God in answering the prayer we offered in the first place!"

"I see," the farmer sighed, his mind striving to memorize the thought as Jesus had expressed it.

"Greetings!"

Wheeling around, Jesus was surprised to see his father, Joseph, standing within feet of where he was standing. His father was smiling, too, and that brought relief to Jesus, as he had worried that he had again taken advantage of the freedom his father had given him.

"Well, Jesus," Joseph said, extending his hand to that of the farmer. "Are you going to introduce me to your new friend?"

"Of course," Jesus exclaimed repentantly. "Father, this is . . . I'm sorry, sir, but I don't believe you told me your name."

"I am Joseph," the man laughed. "Actually I am from Arimathaea, not here where you find me. I was also at the feast, but left early to assist my widowed sister. Her husband died but a fortnight ago, and I came to plant—"

"You see, sir?!" Jesus blurted, interrupting the man. "You likewise know the *key!*"

"What key is this?" Joseph asked. "I'm not sure I follow you, Jesus."

"It's a long story," Jesus answered, smiling first up at this father and then at the other Joseph.

"I see what you mean, Jesus," the man replied. He then did something entirely unexpected. He reached down, drew his arm around the shoulders of Jesus, and said, "I'll remember what you have taught me, son, and I'll remember you, too. If you and your family are ever in Arimathaea, please stay with my family. We have been abundantly blessed with a large home, and we could accommodate you well."

Then Joseph of Arimathaea did something else entirely unexpected. He took several coins from a pocket in his garment. "Take these," he said, placing them in Jesus' cupped hands. "Two mites, or leptons, three quadrans, and a denarius. They're Roman coins, of course, but we use them nonetheless."

Drawing the fistful of coins to his chest, Jesus looked up to his father for approval to accept the gift. Joseph merely nodded, at the same time smiling affectionately down at his son.

"But," the other Joseph continued, winking, "there is one provision upon which I give you this gift. You must use these coins to help any widows you might know in your village. We sometimes overlook these husbandless women, Jesus, and their needs are just as great as ours."

"I promise, sir," Jesus responded, winking back at his benefactor. "And I thank you very much."

"And I thank *you*, Joseph of Arimathaea," Jesus' father added. "You've taught our son well. . . ."

Turning, then, Joseph began walking back to the resting caravan. Thinking that Jesus was following him, he began to talk out into the air, reminding Jesus that he should stay close to the others. His words vanished without being heard, however, for at that moment, Jesus was giving his new friend a giant, childlike embrace.

In parting, Joseph said, "Your thoughtful insights are gratifying to hear, Jesus. It is not often that one listens to the wisdom of a child. For sadly, so many of our younger ones respond to the negative pressures of their peers. They are simply unable to even comprehend the message of compassion and warmth as you have explained them to me. I cannot help but wonder how it is that you are so knowledgeable about life's weightier matters. There is such understanding in your words that you are completely different from other children I have known."

Tenderly, the old man held a firm grip on the Savior's hand, actually caressing it a little as he continued to speak. "Perhaps," he said, "my prayers have been answered. Perhaps it was meant for us to meet. For you see," he continued, wistfully "I had a son, as well . . . a fine, handsome son like yourself. His name was Jabeth. But, when he was your age, instead of listening to the wisdom of his elders and learning from their mistakes, he chose a different path—a path of selfishness. This choice caused a great deal of pain and suffering to himself, as well as to his mother and me . . . before he died."

"Died, sir?" Jesus questioned.

"Yes, my friend, my son Jabeth died. And although the matter still weighs heavy in my heart, I shall only say that had he been a person who looked to the needs of others rather than focusing on his own selfish desires, he would have accompanied me to the Great Feast, then be here today to meet you. My Nazarene friend, how I would have loved for my son to have had a friend like yourself. It may very well have saved his life."

"But, how . . ." Jesus began, wanting to satisfy his curiosity about the matter, ". . . what did he—?" However, before Jesus could finish his thought, his father, Joseph, called out to him, beckoning.

"Go to your father, Jesus . . . we'll meet again, I'm sure. Do not tarry longer. Your father will think I'm a selfish old man . . . which, I suppose, I am."

"Goodbye, Joseph of Arimathaea!" Jesus cried out as he ran down the path, while at the same time holding his clenched fist high into the air. "And thank you again for these coins!"

It was several moments before the old man from Arimathaea could see clearly. He longed to have held his son, as he had held Jesus, and to have been embraced by such strong, young arms. *One day, perhaps,* he thought, *if only Jehovah's atonement can pay for Jabeth's sins. . . .*

The sun was deep in the afternoon sky as the weary travelers wound along the dusty path. It was too much effort to talk, so instead of visiting, Joseph focused his thoughts on the woman at his side. His Mary, he realized, had been endowed with certain gifts from their Heavenly Father. Somehow she seemed able to comprehend matters of the heart in a way that he did not. While he, too, had been blessed with insights—even the dream from the heavenly messenger before his marriage to Mary—Joseph was reverently appreciative of Mary's unique gifts. And though this son, so beloved by Joseph, was not actually the flesh of his flesh or the blood of his blood, he had accepted the calling that was his.

How Joseph wished that his oldest could take his trade and become a carpenter like himself, and his father before him. But Joseph knew that Jesus' life was meant to take a different turn. So now, in keeping with those same sentiments, he simply watched and listened.

While these thoughts played on Joseph's mind, Mary was likewise deep in her own thoughts. As she walked along, she found herself giving thanks to Heavenly Father for yet another fulfilling and reassuring sign that Jesus was a future leader and was rapidly increasing in knowledge and understanding for a purpose that was more clear with each passing day.

As were his parents, Jesus was also deep in thought. Kicking the dust ahead of him, he reflected on the unusual and unexpected meeting with the man called Joseph. Jesus recalled first observing the man as the stranger was planting tiny seedlings into the rich soil. Before being noticed by the farmer, Jesus had seen one seed fall, unnoticed, from the farmer's hand and float silently into a small crack just inside a fair-sized boulder. Jesus knew that the seed would die, for without the proper nourishment and soil in which to expand its roots, its life forces could never come alive.

He noted other such seeds that were also doomed to lifelessness, rather than growth. Still others were quickly eaten by a flock of small birds, and never given a chance to survive. Suddenly a parable was framed inside his mind, one that he would use many times in future days to give example to his teachings.

"The Parable of the Sower," he whispered audibly. "That's what I'll call it. And when I do, I'll remember Joseph of Arimathaea, and the seeds he planted in my heart this very day."

Inwardly, Jesus cried out once more to his Father in Heaven, offering a prayerful thanks for the continued light and knowledge that seemed to fill his heart. Although it was hard for him to imagine, he was the creator of the earth and all its inhabitants. He was the son of God. He was the Christ foretold by the ancient prophets of old. He inwardly rejoiced for those of us who would follow after divine whisperings within our hearts, even as the generous farmer had done. Such devotion, after all, was the object and aim of our existence.

VI

During the next two years, Jesus grew strong and prosperous with his family, returning each day to the routine of the carpenter's shop. He worked hard to become an effective carpenter and builder, just like his father, despite the inward urgency that seemed to compel him in other directions. Nevertheless, he had given a great deal of thought to his initial journey to Jerusalem, and had begun concentrating on ideas that seemed to come into his fertile mind like tidal waves of sheer understanding. He found himself constantly watching and listening to those around him, and wondering why so many people seemed unhappy, while others appeared to take life with ease and indifference.

I have no doubt that as grownups spoke to Jesus, he found it necessary to stifle the urge to correct what he seemed to know in his heart were inaccurate answers. However, in keeping with the laws of the land, he knew that it was better to listen than attempt to correct, even when he knew that he was right and they were wrong. It was a matter of respect. Nevertheless, he was dismayed to learn how quickly others were deceived and misguided.

For this reason, Jesus held to the simple, easy-to-comprehend parables that formed almost daily in his mind. Truth was simple and concise! What better way to teach than with simple examples?

Related to this, Jesus found another gift surfacing, one that he had never considered. Once his stories, or parables, took root inside his head, he never lost them. Indeed, he referred to them often when trying to delicately teach the unteachable.

Men, he discovered, were curious creatures, indeed. Some were honest, some were not. Some were profit seekers, while others seemed content with the simple bounties of God-given blessings. Some men were evil, and went to great lengths to destroy the lives of others. Yet others were peacemakers, and despite the wrongs inflicted on them by others, these men and women would quickly forgive and forget.

Jesus also pondered the story of the wayward son that the farmer, Joseph, had shared with him. While thinking how devastated the old man and his wife must have been at the passing of their eldest child, Jesus experienced a glimpse into the world just beyond the veil, and thought he had actually seen the lad.

"Why?" he whispered, as though Joseph's son, Jabeth, was in his presence. "Why did you not follow the counsel and advice of your caring parents? Why did you think that *your* way was the better way, even though your father and mother had lived so much longer than yourself? And tell me, Jabeth, how could you hurt yourself and those you loved by giving up the way you did?"

He didn't exactly know how he had been able to envision the young lad in his mind, but he somehow knew everything that had happened, and he shed sorrowful tears in the boy's behalf. However, this too, Jesus thought, had the power to be a teaching tool; and though he remained sorrowed at the pain of Jabeth's father and mother, he felt grateful for what he had learned from the man called Joseph of Arimathaea.

In reverence to this memory, Jesus found a place of solitude behind his father's shop. Falling to his knees, he called out to God for direction and support. He knew that even though he, like his fellow man, would feel temptations in his mortal life, he was now even more determined to succeed as he knew his Heavenly Father desired.

After some time, Jesus found his thoughts turning to his friends—at least to those boys who sometimes said they were his friends. These thoughts darkened his soul, and before long he had to arise and ask his mother a question. It was late, anyway, and time to prepare for bed.

Entering the door of their humble home, Jesus went directly to the room to the rear, where Mary had already retired. "Mother," he inquired softly, "the other boys say that I am different, and they don't want to be around me."

Sensing her son's pensive mood, Mary replied, "Of course they want to be with you, Jesus. You are a fine boy. . . ."

"I am seldom asked to join them," Jesus continued, "and at times I am ridiculed for sharing the thoughts that I have."

"I am sure they don't mean to hurt you, Jesus."

"I just wish I could see Lazarus more often, and do things with him. At least Lazarus accepts me the way I am, and respects me."

Mary ran her fingers through her son's tousled locks of hair, and looking right into his eyes, said with conviction, "Jesus, I'm going to tell you something that I have said before. Sometimes in the routine of living it is hard to remember that you are the Son of the Living God—the Holy Messiah. Although Joseph is your father on earth, your real father is the most high God. This makes you different from anyone who has ever lived. You are of royal birth, Jesus! Yes, you are different . . . very different. Yet, you must use this uniqueness to help your friends want to be better—just by doing things with them. I don't want you to miss your childhood, for you will soon be a man. While you are still a child, however, take time to enjoy the friends you have.

"It is late now," Mary continued, "and the sun has passed to the west. Come and lie down, and rest for tomorrow."

"But Mother. . . ."

"Yes, dear one?"

"It hurts when they call me names."

"Children are not the only cruel ones, Jesus. You will be called many things in your life. Just be concerned with what *we* call you, then be true to who you are."

With those words hanging suspended in the air, Mary pulled Jesus's woven blanket up and gently tucked him into bed. Quiet night conversations were some of the most rewarding talks of all. Her voice cracked with emotion as she concluded, "And, although the thought of your calling is almost more than even you can comprehend, even at this early age you can do what Heavenly Father requires of you, no matter the price!"

"I'll try, Mother . . . I really will. But can I ask you a question?"

"Yes, Jesus, what is it?"

"Well, I'm not really sure how to ask it, but do you love Heavenly Father more than you love Father?"

"My, but your mind is growing. Actually, Jesus, I've never thought of comparing my feelings between your two fathers, but I think . . . yes, I would answer this way. I love Heavenly Father in a way that I can't explain, but is consuming and fulfilling. It is because of this love that I am able to love dear Joseph. Joseph is the father of your little brother and sister, you know, and in my mind is the finest man in all of Galilee. So, to answer your question more, I love them both, but in two totally different ways. My feelings for the two do not compete, but rather build upon each other. I am just overwhelmed and humbled to feel of their love for me."

"Thank you, Mother, for sharing your feelings," Jesus sighed. "Although I don't understand all that you said, I will think of your words and learn. But promise me that you'll remember what you just said, then share them with me again when I am older. I really do want to understand what *love* is."

"I think, Jesus," Mary concluded, kissing her son lightly on his cheek, "that you have much more understanding than you know. Now, go to sleep, and in the morning I'll make your very favorite *matzos.*"

"I love you, Mother," Jesus whispered.

"I love you, too, dear Jesus."

As Mary walked from the room, leaving Jesus to enter the world of sleep, a tear of renewed gratitude fell from her cheek. To be the mother of such a son—the Son of God, she considered—was almost more than she could comprehend.

VII

Because the village my family lived in was but an hour's walk from that of Jesus' village, our families grew together, which allowed me to observe my Lord as he explored his awakening identity. What I learned in his presence, as well as from his mother Mary's record, was that Jesus was not easily distracted by the events going on around him. He was never disobedient or mischievous, but he *was* inquisitive, and sought often to understand and be a part of the events that occurred in his home town. Such was the case that very same summer, as our friend Lazarus accompanied a caravan north from Bethany, just to visit him.

I include here an epistle I long ago received from Lazarus.

My good friend Mary,

It seems like years since we laughed and played together. These memories are fond, especially as I consider the singular blessing that was ours to learn and grow at the side of our dearest friend, Jesus. Permit me to share a sacred memory of an event that occurred when I first came to Nazareth, two years after we met at the Feast of the Passover.

The afternoon following my arrival, just outside of Nazareth at a narrow river crossing, Jesus, his friend, Peter, and I were walking along, engaged in conversation. Of a sudden, we saw two bearded bedouin leading their donkeys over to the side of the road. They appeared to be in the process of mending something unseen on one of the saddles. But, as we drew closer to the strangers, Jesus suddenly *knew* that danger was lurking in the desert shadows.

A few yards to the left of the river, an elderly couple Jesus had known for as long as he could remember, was pushing their cart toward the bridge that led into the village of Nazareth. Their small handcart was filled to capacity with goods they apparently intended to sell at their street-front market.

For a moment the youthful Jesus looked into the faces of the two strangers, then back at the approaching couple with their small cart. Immediately, he understood the heart of the ruffian that the second man was calling "Master Barrabus." Instantly Jesus was in flight, racing ahead of the aged couple to make contact with the men. I called out, but to no avail, as Jesus was determined to speak to the bearded strangers and divert them from harming the man and woman.

When Jesus pulled up in front of the men, he discerned their emotions to be both anger and disdain in being interrupted at such a pivotal moment in their scheme.

"Why do you wait for the old couple?" Jesus questioned fearlessly, knowing full well that it was their intent to rob the elderly vendors of their belongings before they could reach the safety of the inner village. "Is it because you think you can prevail over them, and bring them to their knees with your evil deeds?"

The two men stood aghast, staring in disbelief, first at each other, and then at the fearless youth. They were stunned to be approached with such boldness.

"Be gone, boy!" the one called Barrabus shouted angrily. The look in the man's eyes was fierce, and his manner was one of obvious contempt for the youthful Jesus for intervening at such an inopportune moment.

Jesus, however, was not frightened. Instead, he became more determined than ever to divert the thieves before they ruined the lives of the defenseless man and woman.

"It is you and your deceitful friend who must leave!" Jesus countered intensely. "You and your kind are not welcome here in Galilee—unless, of course, you come in peace."

The two robbers stared in disbelief at Jesus, attempting to comprehend his remarkable bravery. They just stood there like two fools, allowing the elderly couple to pass unmolested. Then, in unrestrained anger, Barrabus lunged forward to assault the brave young Nazarene. This act, however, was a useless attempt at revenge; for, without a word, Jesus perceived his thoughts a second time and quickly stepped to one side, causing the man to end up in a heap in the dust beneath him.

Totally frustrated, and incapable of comprehending what powers were before them, Barrabus sat up, looked into the eyes of the youthful Jesus, and cried out, "You're finished, boy! By the gods of heaven, you will pay the price of your interference! You had your chance to leave quietly, but you chose to stick your nose where it did not belong! And now, foolish child of ignorance, you *will pay!*"

"*Silence!*" Jesus retorted fearlessly. "It is not me, but the two of you who will pay for your arrogant ways. How dare you use Father's name in vain, or chastise me for stopping you from committing more of the atrocities of the devils that lurk inside your souls?!"

Again the two men just stood and stared at the resolute Jesus. They couldn't believe they had been beaten by a youngster; yet somehow deep within their souls, they seemed to understand that this was not just some ordinary lad from the west side of Nazareth. To the contrary, he seemed almost *godlike* with powers that were not comprehensible to either of them.

Once again the man Barrabus tried to speak, but Jesus quickly cut him short and said, "In the name of Israel's God, I command you both to leave!"

Without understanding why, the totally angered but beaten men did in fact gather the reins from their beasts of burden. Then, muttering profanities under their breath, they turned and led their animals down the trail and away from the village.

Immediately Jesus retreated to the anxious, aged couple. Giving them each a warm embrace, he bid them farewell. As they silently retreated, he wiped the perspiration from his forehead, then slowly walked down into the solitude of a nearby ravine.

Nearly out of our sight, Jesus slowly retired to a sitting position, then gazed absently at the sand and gravel near his feet. I saw his tears fall to the sand. Conscious of the defiant spirits that railed inside the hearts of the two would-be assailants, Jesus felt pity for their souls. He felt indignation as well, for he knew how completely helpless his elderly friends would have been, had he not intervened. He wondered, as he sat there, how it was that men's hearts could become so callous and indifferent to others around them. He tilted his head upward, and prayed aloud to his Father.

"Thank you, Father," he whispered audibly. "I am but a boy, but I know thou *art* my Father. I also know thou hast heard my prayers. I thank thee for thy help in sending them away and protecting the old couple."

Concluding his prayer, Jesus arose and slowly made his way to Peter and myself. He knew that both of us were confused, and he counseled us not to speak of the matter with anyone.

"But, why?" I asked.

"Because," Jesus said, "when we call upon Heavenly Father and a miracle is wrought, it is not always best to tell others about it. They may be unbelievers and use this same miracle as a way to scoff and ridicule God. We should refrain from casting our pearls before animals that would press the pearls into the dirt beneath their feet.

"For this reason, my friends," Jesus continued, "I ask you to hold your tongues and tell no one what you have seen."

Peter and I glanced quickly at each other, then back at Jesus. Innocently, then, Peter asked, "Just who are you, Jesus? You frighten full-grown men away with your words, yet you are not frightened when doing it."

"Who said I wasn't afraid?" Jesus countered ruefully. The three of us laughed, then turned and began our descent into the village.

As we walked along, I stooped over, picked up a rock, and threw it in the direction of a gnarled Joshua tree.

"That's quite a throw," Jesus laughed.

"Not nearly good enough, however," I replied.

"I wonder," Jesus interrupted, changing the subject, "do you believe what the rabbis teach us about having a loving God?"

"You *know* I do, Jesus," I stated matter-of-factly.

"And what about you, Peter?"

"Well," Jesus' friend began, "I don't really know. I want to believe, but it all seems so . . . well, I'm not sure if I do, or not."

Searching in his young mind for a reply, Jesus finally responded by asking an even deeper question. "What about our Heavenly Father, Peter? Do you understand what it is to have *faith* in God?"

"No . . . not really," Peter sighed.

"I'm not sure I do, either," I admitted.

"To me," Jesus said thoughtfully, "faith in our Heavenly Father is a tool of power that can never be matched. It is the strength within us that allows us to achieve things that we would not otherwise be capable of doing. It is a link between this world and the magnificent world of the heavens where God lives. He has promised that if we will have complete faith in his commands, he will fight on our side in the battles that will rise up around us, and we will emerge victorious!"

"I'm still confused," Peter interrupted. "Explain it some more, Jesus."

"Faith," Jesus continued, his voice gaining strength, "is our ability to believe in that which we can't see with our eyes, or hear with our ears. It is our ability to know, for instance, that God *is* in the heavens, watching over and caring for us, even though we cannot see him.

"Faith in Heavenly Father's protection," Jesus added, "is what gave me the courage to thwart the attack of those two ruffians on the bridge. I knew God was there for me, directing my path. He knew my needs even before I knew them, and for this reason I did not hesitate to call upon him to assist me—and my elderly friends— when we needed him most."

Peter and I marveled at his uncanny wisdom, and looked at each other with newly believing eyes. We somehow *knew* he was right, and if we heeded his words, we would find protection and direction in all we sought to do.

"Thank you, Jesus," Peter suddenly said, breaking the silence between us. "I like what you have told us, and I know it will help me when I grow older."

Discerning once again a future that could not have been seen by any other mortal, Jesus looked into Peter's eyes and said, "Be a believer, Peter, that's all I ask. Just be a believer in the divine powers unseen, and one day you and I will walk again through the streets of the villages, and together we'll bring many to their knees before the Almighty Father."

"*We will?!*"

"Yes, dear friend, we will. Just remember what I told you about faith. *Think* faith, do faith promoting *deeds*, then watch us become the kind of men Heavenly Father expects us to be."

With these words ringing in our ears, Jesus extended his arms, and we walked down off the hill. We were a threesome, arm over arm, and at that moment we felt a *oneness* and *goodness* that was delicious to our youthful souls.

When at last we reached our small village, we patted each other on the backs, then silently went our separate ways—Peter to his home, and Jesus and I to his. The sun was dipping onto the wind-scarred sands to the west, and we each knew that supper would be soon be served.

This concludes my epistle, Mary. I know you will enjoy learning more of our friend Jesus. As always, I look forward to visiting with you again soon, and enjoying some of your delicious leavened bread!

I remain your friend,

Lazarus

As I read back through Lazarus' letter, I think of the irony that my Lord would years later be crucified in place of this same robber, Barrabus.

VIII

From Lazarus, I learned still more of Jesus and the unique friendship they shared. Lazarus was blessed to be invited to stay at the home of Joseph and Mary to attend school with Jesus. Lazarus speaks often of those days, of the mornings in school, of the afternoons in the hills tending the sheep. As Lazarus has described those warm summer days, I can almost feel the sun upon me. It is as if I can hear the Master's voice and see those two young boys, whose lives intertwined with such destiny.

"Jesus!" The voice was a familiar one. "Jesus! Wake up!"

Jesus began to stir, and reluctantly he opened his eyes to see a familiar figure hovering directly over him. "I must have fallen asleep, Lazarus," he said warmly. "I was tending to the wound on Koli's leg, and fell asleep when the sun sank over the sea."

"Koli?" Lazarus queried curiously. "Who is Koli?"

"You've not met Koli?" Jesus asked with a growing smile on his face.

"No," the boy admitted matter-of-factly, "I haven't. Who is he?"

"First," the young Savior said, "Koli is not a 'he.' He's a 'she'!" He pictured the tiny, helpless creature he'd just spent the afternoon with. "Koli," he instructed kindly, "is the name of my uncle's youngest lamb. She was born just three nights past, and was doing well until she stumbled into a dry well at the bottom of that ravine over there." Jesus pointed toward the sea, then signaled for his friend to watch.

"There is a forgotten place down there, Lazarus, where the water refuses to flow. And yet, for some reason, some of my uncle's sheep wander down to the lower, dryer meadows. They search for food that was once a part of the fertile valley beyond that knoll, but cannot seem to understand that the meadows are now dry and barren."

"But, if there is no food or water," Lazarus argued, "what drives them back to that place, Jesus?"

"It is their instinct, I think," Jesus answered, knowing full well that it was so, but not wanting to sound overly knowledgeable. "Many of my uncle's lambs were born down there, and from time to time they seem almost compelled to return."

"Do all of your uncle's sheep have names?"

"Most of them," Jesus answered. "Why do you ask, Lazarus?"

"Who takes the time these days to name and number their sheep, Jesus? With so many tasks to be done, so much to learn, and so little time to do it all, who takes time to count sheep?"

"My uncle does."

"So I see," Lazarus sighed.

"Oh," Jesus countered kindly, "but you do *not* see. You cannot understand the significance of one lonely sheep if you cannot understand the importance of its worth to the shepherd."

Lazarus scratched his head and considered the thinking of his school companion and devoted friend, then turned to the mortal Messiah and helped him to his feet. "You're different, Jesus," he said, not unkindly, to the Nazarene who had already given him so much. "You're not like the other boys in the synagogue. And yet, you don't look any different than the rest. . . ."

"What do you mean, Lazarus?" Jesus asked, not really wanting to draw attention to himself, but already fully aware, as he always was, that there was truth in his friend's words. "Why do you call me different?"

"Well, to begin with," Lazarus pointed out, "those sheep you were referring to—they seem to understand you, Jesus. It's like they know in their hearts that you are their friend, and that you are there for them, no matter what."

"I *am* their friend," Jesus affirmed, "and I do care for them just as I should care for them."

"It's not that you simply *care* for them, Jesus," Lazarus countered. "It's more than that, and you know it."

"What do you mean?"

"I'll tell you what I mean," Lazarus said. "I'm talking about the way they come to you without hesitation, and the way they seem to understand your every command.

"My father—as you well know—has had numerous flocks of game hens and roosting chicks, and through the years I have grown to care for and even love many of them. But never have I seen such a clear display of devotion from any animal. Never! It is like I have said, they think of you as one of their own, the way the newborn considers its parents. The young and old alike are attracted to you, Jesus. You know what I'm talking about. There's something that compels them to follow you, or come to you, when you call out to them. Furthermore, Jesus, you know what it is, don't you!"

For a moment the Son of God considered all that had been observed and alluded to by his inquisitive companion. Inwardly, he thanked the heavens for his friend; for indeed, Lazarus was one of the few individuals he felt he could fully trust in this perplexing and often chaotic world of mortals.

Jesus knew the answers already. He was young, it was true, but was inwardly mature in a way that was incomprehensible to his devout friend. Jesus knew and fully understood why it was that the animals, as Lazarus had so clearly pointed out, had not only sensed his goodness but had innately understood the divine attraction between themselves and their mortal shepherd. But Jesus knew also that the relationship he'd begun to develop with the animals, as well as with those precious human brothers and sisters around him, was being orchestrated by powers unseen. He also knew that for the purposes of the Father, he had been sent to earth for a mission of divine mercy for all creatures.

"Perhaps you are right, my friend," he said to his curious companion. "Perhaps they do think of me as their *parent*."

Jesus felt a sudden warming sensation enter his heart, as he too considered the words he had just spoken, for it was an accurate assessment. He *was* the parent of these sheep before him—at least in a spiritual way. He was indeed the "Creator" of not only the sheep, but of all the animals that roamed the earth, as well.

Always, in the Savior's mind, despite his outwardly youthful appearance, he sought for and took advantage of the many teaching moments that came his way. He was delighted when one of his friends or schoolmates would inquire about matters of a spiritual nature. Likewise, he was at times moved to tears when the right moments would provide those humble recipients with occasional glimpses of what he termed "the gospel."

Lazarus stepped forward and placed his hand on the Savior's shoulder. "I know I'm right," he said calmly, relishing the moments he continued to share with his smarter-than-usual friend. "And I'll tell you something else, Jesus. . . ."

Without saying a word, Jesus waited for his friend to continue speaking.

"You *are* different!" Lazarus declared boldly. "You don't seem to have the same worries as the rest of us. You don't ever quarrel with others. In fact, I don't think I've ever seen or heard you raise your voice in anger at anyone, including your parents."

"Lazarus," Jesus countered softly, "is it different to be one who listens to the words and counsel of our elders, or to the soft commands of our parents? Is it different to be one who studies and wants to learn truths? Is it different to find a place in one's heart for love to grow, and gardens along the way to plant and reap harvests of charitable acts—whether they be directed to those we love, or even to strangers or enemies? And is it unusual to want to provide comfort and even shelter for our animal friends, whose very existence allows us, as human sons and daughters of men, to prosper, and occasionally to even feed and nourish ourselves? I love the creatures who walk the earth, Lazarus, because of their divine origin."

"What are you talking about, Jesus?" Lazarus retorted, stepping back from the young teacher.

"They are the Father's animals, Lazarus," Jesus affirmed, casting a momentary glance heavenward. "Created by him, loved by him, and individually numbered by his matchless powers, for the purposes of his understanding. And if they be his, then ought we not to love them even more? Are they not gifts to us from him?"

"Well," Lazarus mumbled shakily, "I suppose so, but. . . ."

"If the animals of the earth are numbered and obviously important to our Father, then how much more important are we to him who created us?"

"You sound like a rabbi, Jesus," Lazarus concluded, "but you sure don't look like one! For a moment there, I pictured you with the sacred writings of the Torah and thought you'd do well as a replacement for the aging Agabus."

The two boys chuckled, remembering the old teacher who'd taught them in the synagogue the week before. He was a wise old man, with a tender heart and a clear disposition for charity. The two young boys had equal respect for his teachings because of it.

"Remember how Agabus cried right in front of the class, Lazarus? Remember how he instructed us to open our hearts to all of the pleas for help that seemed to continually surround us? To reach out to the poor and needy, to give of ourselves even if it meant that we might very well go without? And remember how he helped us learn those concepts in a way that no other instructor could? You can't say that you didn't feel the same kinds of feelings most of us in the classroom felt. There was a definite spirit there, Lazarus. It was a feeling that seemed to come into our hearts and tell us that he was a good man, a responsible man, who not only understood the concepts he taught, but who reached out to us in such a way as to be able to pass the message of hope directly into our hearts."

"You're right, Jesus," Lazarus confirmed, thinking back to one experience in particular that had so touched him that he too had been unashamed when the tears had come. "Of course I remember feeling peaceful in Rabbi Agabus' class. It was just last week. But, that still doesn't answer my question."

"Your question?"

"Yes, good friend, my question. We were talking about *your* abilities, not the teaching techniques or attributes of Rabbi Agabus."

"I'm not sure I follow. . . ."

"But you must, Jesus," Lazarus insisted. "You're like the old rabbi right now, because you seem to know all of the answers. Now, I might be younger, Jesus, but I'm not a fool. There is something different about you, and you know it as well as I do.

"Who are you, Jesus?" Lazarus pressed, sensing that he was making headway with his constant probing. "Who are you that you can raise your hand at every question, and even know the answers to questions before they are asked? Who are you, Jesus, that you can cause herds of mindless animals to come your way at the simple command of your voice, or that when someone is ill or in need, you do not hesitate to be there for them? Who are you, Jesus of Nazareth? Are you really just the carpenter's son?"

Lazarus leaned against a nearby log, recalling the time when his friend, Jesus, had fashioned a sturdy walking stick, then passed it along to an aged, crippled friend. "I think that you are more than the simple son of a carpenter, Jesus, because you *care*. You just plain *care*. Mark my words, Jesus, there will come a day when others will see you like I do. Others will know you as the great teacher that you are."

Jesus responded quietly, "In God's eyes, aren't we all different—unique and special, with our own talents and abilities, our own missions to fulfill?"

Jesus arose and walked two steps over to where his young, energetic friend was standing. He placed a friendly hand on top of the boy's shoulder and said, "You're my best friend in the whole world, Lazarus. You, *too*, are a teacher. You, *too*, have the spirit of our Father within your breast . . . and I feel honored that you consider me to be your friend. I will not hesitate to be there for you, too, if you need me, no matter how far apart we become, or what directions we take in life. You will always be my friend."

"And you mine," Lazarus confirmed. "Friends to the end of time!"

IX

Three months later, on the sixth day of April, Jesus awakened bright and early. It was his fifteenth birthday, and as he did so often, he went out into the morning sunlight to a place where he delighted in being completely alone. He'd had a dream during the night, a distant far-off place. It felt strangely like a forgotten past life, one in which he had been taught and schooled.

As Jesus nestled into his favorite sitting spot, he broke a weed off by the stem, then rolled it again and again in his mouth. He reasoned that the dream he'd had was nothing more than a subconscious silhouette, like so many others of which he'd been a part. But the face of the man in this dream had been a familiar one—very familiar.

"But, who was he?" Jesus heard himself saying, trying desperately to make the unlikely connection in his mind. His mental searching, however, was to no avail; for after every line of thought had entered his mind, a definite blank was drawn.

After a short but strenuous time had passed, Jesus gave up altogether and tried to forget the faceless image. Even so, his mind kept coming back to the man, and he found himself probing his memory for clues as to the man's identity.

Jesus knew there was only one way to resolve his discomfort, and he knelt and offered a brief but earnest prayer.

In silence he sat, waiting for an answer. When nothing came to mind, he pressed his memory for details. All at once, and without warning, into his mind came a glimpse of a particular moment in time that was startling—

Darkness was upon the land. While he realized the scene was mid-day, an immense shadow hung over the earth, and people everywhere were in serious distress, calling out in mighty prayer for relief.

Deep within his heart, Jesus anguished with these people, for he knew not what had engulfed the region. In addition to this dismal spell of evil, Jesus felt an agonizing pain that he had never before experienced. This pain pulsated through his hands and feet, and as he lifted his arms in an attempt to understand, he was given to know the ultimate sacrifice that he would be called upon to make.

Trepidation crept into Jesus' heart, for he had never experienced so profound an image of terror. Yet before he could ask the question "Why?" his heart was filled with an understanding that consumed his entire being. He was going to lose his life so that all mankind might return to the Father, in spite of their sins! He was going to be subjected to the angry masses who could not, or would not, understand his mission of peace. They would, at some point in time, sentence him to die a painful, agonizing death upon a wooden cross!

A wooden cross?!

For a brief moment, Jesus felt his mortal heart beating faster than it ever had before. Although he realized that the brutal sacrifice was to be carried out some time in the years to come, he felt pain nonetheless, and experienced a great sorrow in his heart.

Jesus rose to his feet, looked all around him, then walked out of the field and onto an old dirt road which led to the outskirts of Nazareth. He was tired and strangely cold at the same time.

Was it really so? Would he actually be lifted on a wooden cross and left there to die for no other reason except that he had been compelled to tell the truth of who he was?

Troubled by the horrifying insight he had seen regarding his future, Jesus cried aloud for comfort. "Father, why must I endure this agony? Is this the mission you sent me forth to accomplish? Am I to spend all the days of my life recruiting followers of thy word, only to be smitten down and destroyed in the flesh?"

For a moment there was only silence. But then, quite unexpectedly, Jesus heard a distinct voice pierce the very center of his soul.

"Be of comfort, my Son . . . I will forever be with thee."

The words gave comfort to Jesus. He needed no more than his Father's love, and so he simply basked in the echo of the words. Peace! Peace at last!

Still, there was that almost familiar face from his dream. "Who was it?!" he whispered to himself.

Pensive and anxious, Jesus turned a corner at a small alleyway and walked southward through the narrow street. As the shadows of the buildings paraded past him, Jesus suddenly remembered his promise to help his father in the carpenter's shop.

He turned homeward, winding his way back through the maze of dirt-lined streets and alleys. Once at home, he immediately entered his father's shop.

"Good morning, son," Joseph exclaimed. "Good health to you on this birthday!" Then, looking at his son more closely, he saw that Jesus was troubled. "What's wrong, Jesus? What's happened?" Joseph asked.

"Oh," the young Savior sighed, "nothing important, really."

"Come on, Jesus," Joseph pressed, setting his awl down on the bench before him. "I know you better than that. Please, tell me what troubles you."

Desperately wanting to turn to his father for comfort, Jesus began to explain the dream. Before he could explain completely, however, he thought better of it, and ended the discussion. After all, what good would it do to worry his dear earthly parents, especially if it was a matter for him, and him alone, to deal with? And so, Jesus said only that he'd had some sort of frightening dream.

Instantly Joseph was reminded of the time, almost sixteen years earlier, when he too had experienced a prophetic dream. In this dream, he had learned of Mary's pregnancy and the part he was to play in the rearing of this Son of God. That dream was likewise troublesome for Joseph, for his virtue would be questioned at the moment his betrothed Mary began to physically show that she was "with child." But he had exercised faith as never before, had grown in his faith, and had at last gained a full measure of peace.

Joseph suggested that Jesus call upon God for direction.

"I did that," Jesus exclaimed, although he did not tell Joseph that he had actually heard the voice of his Father in his heart. "Even so, I could not understand certain aspects that were troubling to me."

"Can you tell me, son?" Joseph inquired.

"I saw the face of a man. He seemed to know who I am, but I did not know him. Everything around us was dark."

"It does sound troubling," Joseph said, "but in time peace will come. Do not let it trouble you further. And now," Joseph said in an attempt to distract his son, "we have this table to take across town, and I'm going to need you to help me push the cart. So, are you going with me?"

"Yes, sir," Jesus replied, somewhat lifted in spirits, "I am."

Yet, even with these words, the youthful Savior knew there was more to the dream than mere imagination. And, although he chose not to tell his father about the awful crucifixion that he had seen with such clarity, he was also disturbed about the faceless man and could not let the matter rest in his heart.

An hour later, as Joseph and Jesus carefully transported their newly fashioned table into the home of its new owner, Jesus wiped away the perspiration that still lingered on his forehead. Then, while his father concluded the business he had with the man inside, Jesus sat down outside the front door of the adobe dwelling, and thought—

Absently, he reached down and picked up a small pebble beneath his left foot. He tried again to envision the man in his dream, and was suddenly startled at the sound of a voice beside him.

"Excuse me," the voice said. "Are you from the region?"

"Yes," Jesus looked up and responded cordially to the stranger, "I am. How can I be of help you, sir?"

The man before him was not much older than he—maybe eighteen or nineteen years of age. He was dressed in the typical layered garb common to the travelers in the region, and he carried a small bundle on his back. Jesus surmised that the man was merely traveling through the area, and needed a place to spend the night.

"Well," the man said, "I've been on the road for several days now, trying to reach the Sea of Galilee. They tell me this sea contains the finest fishing in all the land. However, I've no money left in my purse, and am in dire need of nourishment. Could your family spare a morsel of bread for a weary traveler?"

"This is not my home," Jesus replied honestly, "but I will gladly ask my friend who lives here for food."

Excusing himself, Jesus disappeared into the house, then returned moments later with a loaf of bread and some fresh cheese.

"Here," he offered, "take these. They will last you for two or three meals, and if you continue on your journey to the northeast, then you will reach Mount Tabor before nightfall. The Sea of Galilee is beyond that, and you will easily arrive there by noon on the morrow."

The bearded stranger took the generous gifts of food from Jesus, thanking him with a nod of his head. "What is your name, young Nazarene?" he then inquired.

"I am called Jesus," the young Savior replied.

"Well, young Jesus, I am certainly grateful for the food. Please thank your friends for their kindness. Had I any money, I would gladly repay them."

"There's certainly no need for that, my friend," Jesus said. But the stranger's face. . . .

"I am Judas Iscariot, from Kerioth," the man replied politely. As he spoke, he tore a piece of fresh bread and stuffed it into his mouth. "Again, I thank you for your kindness, Jesus. Perhaps we will meet again some day, and I shall have the silver wherewith to show my thanks."

"Good day," Jesus replied awkwardly; for as the man turned away, Jesus suddenly knew the face in the dream, and trembled slightly as the man walked away into the afternoon sunshine.

X

The shadowed face of Judas Iscariot was perplexing and somewhat troubling for Jesus, and during the following night he saw the image over and over in his mind. Initially, he had supposed that as soon as the man's identity had been made clear to him, the images would fade and be laid to rest. Once more, however, as night descended upon his home, Jesus alone found solace in a remote corner of his father's shop—and there poured out his heart to God.

First and foremost, he wanted to know what was to become of him. He understood much, but he was not totally sure of the ultimate outcome of his mortal ministry. Would people listen to his message? Would his time be well spent, so as not to offend his Father? More importantly, would the teachings he cherished live on in the hearts of men following his death?

"Dear Father," he cried out into the darkness of the room, "please, if it be thy will, help me to understand why the man, Judas, came to me in my dream. Help me to understand clearly what thou wouldst have me do, that I might not be frightened away when the time comes for me to once again leave this world and pass into thy presence."

In his search for peace, the youthful Christ cried out to God for answers, although no explanation was given. Realizing that prayers were not always answered on his own timetable, Jesus finally arose, went into the house, and retired to his bed. Almost immediately, despite his troubled heart, he was fast asleep.

The following week was filled with chores for Jesus to perform around the shop and in the village, for he had many deliveries to make for his earthly father.

Nevertheless, like all young men, he also found moments to gather with his friends. More often than not, these gatherings resulted in his sharing newly discovered parables that dealt with human relationships. How we delighted in those moments spent with him!

One day, after the others had been called home, I had a few moments alone with him and I felt to ask him, as I had at the Feast of the Passover, why God had allowed the angel of death to take the lives of so many young children.

Jesus was quiet and did not answer right away—a trait I had often noticed in him as so many young people our age were always ready with quick, though not always intelligent, answers.

But once again I was to be made to wait, for in those moments an elderly woman stumbled across the dirt road. She did not appear to be a village woman, and we saw as she approached us haltingly that she was nearly blind. Her appearance also caused me to jump to my feet and back away. "Jesus," I warned, "the woman. . . ."

The woman was a leper.

Her clothes were rags, her hands mere fingerless stubs of flesh and bone. Likewise, her face was worn and gnarled.

"Poor woman," Jesus whispered, watching closely and with concern as she tried to petition passersby for help. But they drew back in horror. I stood filled with terror as Jesus motioned me to wait for him. He stepped toward the woman and spoke quietly to her.

She seemed to smile and I heard the words ". . . carpenter's son." I saw Jesus nod and incline his head toward the woman. I could not hear them speak as I was too far away, and I waited, wondering what Jesus could do for this poor outcast woman. Lepers were seldom seen in villages; they lived apart from others, in leper colonies. My mother often took food to the colonies and I had helped her, although we saw no one as they hid themselves from us. My mother had simply left the food for them in a basket on the ground. "Will they get it?" I had asked. And my mother had assured me that they would.

I wondered what had made this woman so bold that she would come into the village, where she was sure to be shunned. It was almost as if she had come looking for something or someone. *She was lucky to have come within sight of Jesus,* I thought to myself. *He knows everyone in the village and is well thought of. Surely he will be able to help her find what she needs.*

I watched how Jesus, with the tenderness of a mother holding a newborn babe, lifted his hands toward the woman's face and touched her gently on both cheeks. He then placed his fingers on her forehead. I thought perhaps she might be in need of cool water, so I called to him.

"Jesus!"

But he did not seem to hear me, and I hesitated to call again.

And then suddenly, the woman seemed to sway and I thought she would fall, but Jesus quickly reached out a hand to steady her. She seemed to glow with peace as Jesus continued to speak softly to her. Then, in minutes, Jesus was once again beside me and the woman was gone.

"Who was she?" I asked. "What did she want?"

"A woman who helped my mother many years ago," he said softly. "Her name was Shanna."

I met her myself, not long after the crucifixion. She was there that day, too, she told me, although I did not see her in the crowd. It was not until then that I learned why she had come to Nazareth, and that she had come from the faraway village of Dan. This is the story she told me.

"My name is Shanna, of the tribe of Menassas. At one time, my husband and I ran a prosperous inn in Bethlehem. However, when we became ill we lost the inn and were cast out of town. We found homes in Dan, where lepers are permitted to live on the outskirts of town. My husband and I tried to keep our children away from our presence, but could not. Each of us suffered more than we thought possible. We were dying, one at a time . . . all of us together, because of this accursed disease.

"I was told in a dream to come here to Nazareth, where I would find the assistance of a young man . . . *a carpenter's son.* I was promised that I would not die, and I was instructed that if I placed my faith in the promised Messiah, my family would be healed.

"My husband and I knew that the Messiah had come, because on the night he was born a beautiful star appeared in the heavens like magic in the skies. A beautiful young couple stopped in our small inn, in Bethlehem, to spend the night. That night a child was born. I myself held the infant in my arms. I didn't know it then, but learned shortly thereafter that a great prophecy had been fulfilled. We knew when the magis and the shepherds continued to come for weeks after.

"And so I went to Nazareth to find Jesus. I asked him to heal me, and I was healed."

"And your family?" I asked her.

"They too were healed," she said, weeping.

XI

I was perhaps fifteen when Lazarus was badly injured by one of the family animals. He was tending her when something startled her, and she reared up and kicked him violently in the leg. For some weeks he could not walk, and when he rose from his bed, he walked with difficulty and a limp.

Nevertheless, his family and mine planned a special trip to Nazareth to visit with the family of Jesus, and Lazarus assured them he could make the trip.

When Jesus stepped out from the shop, his concern for Lazarus was immediately evident.

"How are you, Lazarus? What happened?"

Lazarus spoke bitterly, "The donkey kicked me."

"What do the physicians say?" Jesus inquired compassionately.

"They say the damage was great, and that I will never walk or run properly again."

"I am so sorry, my friend." Perhaps Jesus wished to use the healing powers that we would later learn were his. After all, he had no dearer friend than Lazarus! But Jesus' mother, Mary, had cautioned him as a youth, instructing him to use the gifts only when called upon by the Holy Spirit. Jesus considered the staff Lazarus had used to help him on his journey. Twisting it in his hand, he contemplated sadly the poor workmanship of the piece.

"Where did you get this?" he inquired.

"I found it near a well, in Bethany."

"Let me give you a real staff, my friend . . . one that I have just crafted, and that will last for years to come."

"That's not necessary, Jesus. I'm—"

"I know it's not," Jesus interrupted, "but it will be my gift to you. You shall have it to support you all the days of your life."

"You are a true friend, Jesus. And if you do choose to give me such a staff, I shall treasure it always. Thank you."

"Count on it, my friend. Count on it."

That same afternoon, while Joseph and Mary enjoyed the company of our parents, the five of us set out on an adventure. The promised staff had given new life to Lazarus, and he now seemed eager to accompany the rest of us down to the waters of the Kishon River tributary, and swim in the hot afternoon sun.

There was a place along this tributary that Jesus had come to know well. It had first been introduced to him by his parents several years earlier. Since then, he had spent many long afternoons there, basking away the hours in the warm sun. The remote area was a splendid water hole, and offered not only a fresh stream from which to drink, but had also provided him with a chance to cool his feet and ponder the future that was his.

Lazarus and his sisters began whispering and giggling amongst themselves. Then, simultaneously turning to face the perplexed Jesus, they told him something that made his heart leap for joy.

"We're moving," Lazarus grinned.

"You're what?!"

"That's right, Jesus, we're leaving Bethany for good. We are moving right here to Nazareth, and will be near you and your family."

"Can this be true?" Jesus exclaimed. "Moving?!"

"Yes, Jesus," Martha interjected. "Father was offered a new teaching position right here in your synagogue, and he decided to take it."

"Really?!"

"Really!" her sister Mary added. "And, part of the reason your parents let us come to the river today was so that we could be the ones to tell you!"

"Why, that's wonderful," Jesus exclaimed. "That's the greatest news I've heard in months!"

"Well," Lazarus continued, "it won't be until next season, mind you; but by this time next year, we'll all be attending the same synagogue, learning together."

"That means I'll be closer to the three of you, as well," I added. "As you know, it is but an hour's journey from here to Magdala, and I'm sure Father will let us get together often."

That afternoon, as we rested in the sun, Jesus spoke to us of the power of love, and of friendship, a power built upon kindness, and upon each of us becoming "benevolently blind" to one another's weaknesses.

He spoke of the beauty of the world, and yet of its cruelty because so many of our Father's children "break themselves" against his laws. Because of this, he said, we must each resolve to keep our hearts and hands pure, then to stand joyously at each other's side during our respective trials.

"Be not afraid," Jesus concluded, looking at us each directly in our eyes. "My love for you is true, and is undefiled before God."

We knelt and offered a prayer of thanks, of love, and of hope, and I confess that my eyes could not remain closed. For, as my Lord spoke to his Father—to *our* Father—tears slipped down his face, and it was at this moment that I, a peasant girl from Magdala, knew of my own destiny. I would stand at my Lord's side, would minister to him in times of need, and would give my all to his mortal ministry. These thoughts, and the emotions that accompanied them, caused my soul to sing what I would later come to understand as "the song of his redeeming love."

At the conclusion of Jesus' prayer, the five of us stood, embraced, and wept joyously for the new and lofty bond that was now ours. We then splashed in the stream and visited, feeling a sense of oneness that would unite our hearts into the eternities. For Jesus, the antici-pation of having us nearby seemed to be a balm that he would come to rely upon. We would make every effort to be his strength in the years to come, and our homes would be his respite, his havens of rest.

———————————

And so begins the story of my Lord's mortal life. As I recorded at the beginning of this parchment, 67 years have passed since my Lord's birth. I have spent the final half of these years in quiet and lonely reflection, trying to comprehend the power of his atonement and his glorious resurrection from the dead.

In the months ahead, if I am blessed with good health, I will continue the tale on a second set of leather parchments. There I will describe, as best I am able, the years of my Lord's formal ministry.

Until then, I am,

Mary of Magdala.

Part Three
THE TEACHER

Thirty Miles West of Jerusalem, Israel — December 15, 1994

Perspiration streamed down my face and neck. Here I was, a doctoral candidate and translator—yet one fortunate enough to be completing a final, elective class at the university. It was just an hour past noontime, yet my muscles ached as though I had been working for the entire day. My fellow graduate students and good friends, Sid Pershings and Melissa Jones, had been working with me at the dig for past two days. For all three of us, this overnight expedition was a much needed break from our studies.

"So, Jason," Sid paused to reflect as he wiped his brow, "from what Rabbi Cohen said, the Philistines truly were a warlike people."

"Well," I replied, "they sure came with authority, regardless of their technique of conquering this rich Mediterranean lowland. I know our final exam will include the five major cities they had re-established after conquering. These were Ashdod, Gaza, Ashkelon, Gath, and of course Ekron, where we're digging."

"Rabbi Cohen," Melissa agreed, "isn't one to cut corners in his expectations, is he, Jase?"

"Not hardly, Melissa," I replied. "I think he'll want us to track the Philistines, who, during a huge power vacuum in the Mediterranean, came here from Greece. These were the same peoples that Homer wrote of in *The Iliad*. In fact, in reading Homer's works, one sees a parallel with young David's fighting with the Philistine Goliath. You see, it was an accepted practice for the leaders of the respective armies to battle one-on-one to determine the outcome of the entire conflict. Of course, if I know the good rabbi, he won't even deal with the skirmish between young David and that over-fed Philistine!"

We all laughed, then continued our conversation.

"What about this ancient olive oil plant we're excavating, Jason?" Sid asked. "Think he'll hit us hard on it?"

"I really don't know, Sid, but I do think we'll have to expound on the fact that it was the largest olive oil production plant in the Middle East. And to think it was in operation 2,600 years ago! That just blows my mind!"

Just then, as I picked at the ground about four inches below the surface, I unearthed the corner of what proved to be a large, crudely decorated pottery shard. "Not bad, huh, guys?" I asked, holding up the ancient piece of pottery.

"Keep digging, Jase," Melissa teased. "With your luck, you'll find the rest of the container it came from."

Then, as Sid and Melissa resumed their labors, my mind considered the word "luck" that Melissa had used to describe my continual good fortunes. What neither she nor Sid knew, of course, was that the following day I hoped to put a final polish to the first set of scrolls written by Mary Magdalene.

As I thought of this monumental project, which had begun just three months earlier, I could hardly believe the progress I had made. I had spent the first week, with Rabbi Cohen sitting at my side, becoming adept at the translation process. This I had done by first reading and comparing the already translated portions of the scrolls with the Hebrew originals. Once this had been completed, he had pronounced a "blessing" on my apparent competency, and I was on my way. Now, after only ninety days, the rough draft was completed, and I was preparing for my final written exams at the university.

In considering the pace I had maintained, I could hardly comprehend my increased capacity—not only to produce, both with my last formal classes and with the beginnings of my dissertation, but also to handle the added level of stress. These were days never to be forgotten, and because I had maintained full integrity by not sharing my experience with others, I had grown to totally savor the privacy and profundity of the project. The rigors of it had likewise allowed me to brush aside the pain of loneliness and anger that still lay unsettled in my heart. While there had been times during the translating that I had felt the nearness of Kirsten's spirit, still my heart was racked with disquieting emotion.

On a positive note, however, a bonus I had not anticipated had been the daily experience I had enjoyed—that of going into Rabbi Cohen's home, and being "adopted" by the good professor, his beautiful wife, Sarah, and his children, Joseph and Rebecca. They had become as family to me, and had fed me more exotic meals than I could imagine.

In short, the semester had been one of change and growth, one of unresolved pain, and one of loving and being loved. Somehow, in looking back, it now seemed more like a series of competing dreams than reality. It was almost as though the Lord had given me the opportunity to translate as a compensating measure, to counter-balance the loss of my wife. In all, I was most grateful.

The following evening, while my fellow classmates tended to their weekly letter-writing and clean-up, I found myself living the reality of what I had dreamed of the day previous. Here I was, in the private study of Professor Eli Cohen, the most esteemed Hebrew translator in the world. My project was a miracle, to be sure, but one that literally transpired after months of learning and translating at the feet of Rabbi Cohen.

"Well, my American scholar," the good rabbi said in his faint Hebrew accent, "if you are up to it, I would like you to translate the final thought of the story."

Without reply, I examined the ancient Hebrew lettering in context, then read the final words of Mary Magdalene.

"You see," the Rabbi whispered, "the story concludes beautifully."

"Yes, Rabbi, to be sure! But—"

"But *what*, Jason? What is it that puzzles you?"

"You know me well, Rabbi, for indeed I *am* troubled. I understand all that you have shared with me, and especially the profoundness of our project. But, what I *don't* understand is why you—a Jewish rabbi—would feel such affinity for a . . . a *Christian* story. I hope I'm not inappropriate, Rabbi, but it just doesn't *equate.*"

"But Jason," the scholar contested, his face flushed with emotion, "it is *history!* I learned tolerance for the Christian tradition nearly four decades ago, as my father sent me to Oxford University in England. This education was largely criticized by other Jewish scholars at the time; but still he was insistent that I broaden my education at that center. It was his impression that spending four years there would only increase my effectiveness as a rabbi . . . for, not only would I be learning English, but I would gain an understanding for Western thought and culture."

"And what about the Church of England, Rabbi . . . and the *Christian* way of thinking? Did not part of your education have an impact on you . . . on your *heart?*"

"I . . . I'm not sure what you mean, Jason."

"Just this, Rabbi. You, yourself, have often spoken of the Holy Spirit, and your belief in the coming Messiah. You have likewise spent a lifetime pondering the origin of the story that was found by your father. In addition, you have spent the past several months— every spare hour, I might add—helping me translate words and experiences from the youthful Jesus. Has not the Holy Spirit borne witness to your heart that this Jesus was . . . *is* the very Messiah your people are searching for? After all, Rabbi, if what we have translated is true, then Jesus *did* become the Christ . . . and both you *and* I have a conviction of his power."

As my words lingered in the air, I could see a change taking place—not only in the spirit of the moment, but in the Rabbi's eyes—his moist, water-filled eyes. "I have much to think of, my friend" he said, "and will do so this night. Now, do you recall the grove of olive trees we entered last fall, as we were beginning our project?"

"Certainly, Rabbi. I have since then returned to that spot often."

"Fine. Then it is settled. I shall request that you meet me there promptly at 6:00 in the morning . . . that is, if you haven't anything more pressing to attend to."

I looked questioningly at Rabbi Cohen, wondering why our

conversation was so quickly concluding, and wondering as well what such an unusual meeting would lead to.

"But, of course," I answered, using his same backward sentence structure. "Before the sunrise, it will be."

Gesturing with his hand for me to leave, Rabbi Cohen then turned in his chair and dismissed me from his mind and from his home.

The following morning, after a near-sleepless night, I dressed quickly. Then, silently opening the door to my room, I donned my now worn and weathered baseball cap, then slipped outside, allowing my roommate, Sid, to continue his dreams.

Moments later, after winding my way along the base of the Mount of Olives, I arrived at the orchard identified as our rendezvous point, then entered while reverently removing my cap. Within a matter of seconds I found myself staring at Rabbi Cohen; only he was not sitting down, as I expected. Instead, he was kneeling, leaning back on his haunches, and looking very drained and haggard.

"Please . . ." he gestured, inviting me to sit down before him. "It is good to see you, Jason. . . ."

Responding quickly to his request, I settled on a patch of uncut grass, then waited for him to speak.

"It has been a very long night, my American friend."

The rabbi's words hit me squarely as I gazed into his shadowed eyes.

"How long have you been here?" I asked nervously, sensing I was treading on sensitive ground.

"Since you left me last evening," the rabbi sighed. "This mount, as you know, was the ancient olive garden called Gethsemene. . . ."

"Yes, Rabbi, the place where Jesus spent his own night, beginning the atoning process for our sins."

"That is just the problem, Jason—I *see* this! I am experiencing emotions that have never before entered my heart.

"Now," he continued, pushing my mind to the limit, "let me be personal for a moment. I must ask that you *heal me,* Jason! My heart is being rent in two. I am a broken man. Where is my peace, my joy?"

"Rabbi, as you stated, on this same hill Jesus Christ became the 'eternal healer.' If I can be so bold, sir, you are *not* being torn apart, as you suggested, but are actually experiencing a welding back together—the healing that you seek."

"But, Jason, I feel like the olive, after all of its oil has been pushed through the press. The mental pressure I feel at this moment seems to be consuming—"

Then, with his unfinished sentence ringing in the air, Rabbi Cohen did something that was totally unexpected. His mouth grimaced, his hands flew up to cover his face, and he began to sob, burying his covered face in his lap.

For a long moment I sat there, my own emotions and testimony causing my heart to beat wildly. I knew what *I* was feeling, and I also *hoped* to know what Rabbi Cohen was feeling.

At last, as the Rabbi's heaving chest began to settle, he raised his head while at the same time removing his hands from his face. Tears bathed his face, and his eyes . . . his eyes reflected a light and peace that was impossible for me to describe.

"Jason . . . dear, dear Jason. *I know!* I know the ancient parchment speaks truth from the dust. Your Jesus . . . my Jesus was not merely a great teacher, as I have been taught. Nor was he simply the carpenter's son. Mary's very designation feels shallow, almost demeaning. He was . . . *IS the promised Messiah! This I know with my entire being!*"

As Rabbi Cohen spoke, my heart felt as though it would explode. The miracle had transpired, the miracle of conversion that had impassioned my prayers for the months of our working. At that instant, I couldn't wait until I told my friends, Sid and Melissa, for I knew their prayers had been answered, as well.

"But," the rabbi continued, now gazing down at his shaking hands, "with this knowledge comes a realization that creates a further question. How can I respond to my feelings, Jason? There is just no way for me to turn."

Sensing the gut-wrenching realization of what the Rabbi's testimony meant to his future—not only his rabbinical profession, but his acknowledged position as the leader of his extended family and friends—my own heart sorrowed deeply.

Then, just as suddenly as these emotions crept into my soul, a *peace* that passed all understanding consumed my entire being. At the same moment, the morning sun burst over the Mount, illuminating the face of the man who had become my dearest friend. I knew! I knew what I must tell him!

"Rabbi," I whispered, my eyes filling with my own tears, "the Savior, Jesus Christ, *knows* you. Even more important, he loves you . . . for you now love *him.* I don't know the answers of your future, for they are not mine to know. But I *do* know your present, and I have faith that the Savior will not only claim you as his adopted son, but will guide your footsteps into the future."

"Oh, Jason," the rabbi sighed, now smiling for the first time since I had arrived, "you began as my student, yet now you become my teacher. How shall I ever repay you?"

"You don't have to, Rabbi, you just need to—"

"I have it!" the man exclaimed, cutting me off. "I have the solution! Likewise, I have a confession to make for something deceptive that I told you. . . ."

"Excuse me, sir?" I asked, not knowing how to respond.

"I told you only a partial truth last fall, Jason, when we met at John Mark's home. As I recall, I told you that I had located a gift for you . . . a gift of these ancient scrolls. In actuality, my father found *two* ancient relics—two gifts from God—when he unearthed the hidden depository. . . ."

Then, without finishing his thought, Rabbi Cohen reached down, picked up his staff, and extended it to me. Still not fully understanding, my mind focused on the fact that this elderly rabbi was known by the gnarled stick that assisted him wherever he walked. In a way, it was his *signature,* and according to tradition, had been so for as long as anyone could remember.

"Here, Jason . . . this is the staff he found with the Christian scrolls. There is a name, inscribed in Hebrew, along the upper grip, and I thought you would like to translate this name—"

"A name?!" I questioned, not wanting to dwell on what I was thinking.

"Yes, and as you can see, it is written in the same ancient Hebrew dialect you have been learning."

Silently then I pushed my finger along the worn, but still distinct marks as they had been carved along the staff. In a way I was not surprised when the name *LAZARUS* appeared, causing my mind to immediately retreat into the translated pages of the manuscript before me.

"You don't mean—?"

"That this staff, and the one the youthful Jesus fashioned then gave to his friend Lazarus, are *one and the same!* It is so, Jason, and is the very reason that my father and I had to stop translating the scrolls. For, we had both translated enough to know, with certainty, the historical authenticity of the ancient staff and scrolls.

"But, what's more important, Jason, is the symbolism of the staff. It has been a support, both for ancient Lazarus and for myself. But . . . it has also become the support for me to know, without doubt, that Jesus Christ is the 'staff' of life! He is my Redeemer, Jason . . . *our* Redeemer, and as you said, it is with faith that I now walk into my future. There *is* no other way. For you, Jason, perhaps it will help you to walk more uprightly—to be healed of the pain that still festers within your heart."

"Perhaps," I sighed, immediately retreating into the void I had felt since Kirsten's death. I was ashamed of my own lack of faith, yet appreciative of the rabbi's sensitive gesture.

"Now, my young Christian brother," he concluded, seeing that his words had hit home, "we must be going. My Sarah knows of my quest, and is praying that I might come to know truth. She has already disclosed her own belief in Christ—which disclosure, I might add, at first brought great sorrow to my heart. But I must now share my feelings with her, then together we will explore what that means for us. From where I now stand, there is no solution for me and my family—not in this life, anyway. Even so, I will feel of your prayers, Jason, and will pray, myself, that the God of the heavens will understand my unresolvable position. . . ."

As Rabbi Cohen's words trailed off, I somehow sensed that any reply would be ill-timed. I thus remained silent as he slowly arose, then walked silently down the garden path. In his hand he held nothing; while in mine, gripped tightly, was my new staff, made by the young Jesus—*our* Savior and King.

ABOUT THE AUTHORS

Brenton Yorgason is a native of Utah and has served in the U.S. Army in Vietnam. He received a Ph.D. in Family Studies, and has owned and managed several businesses. He has authored or co-authored over forty books, with total sales of well over one million copies. He and his wife, Margaret, are the parents of nine children and reside in Sandy, Utah.

Richard Myers was born and reared in Santa Monica, California. He lived in Italy for two years and is presently completing a bachelor of science degree in psychology. A father of five, Richard and his wife, Susan, reside in Hawaii.

Previous to this work, Brenton and Richard co-authored the bestsellers, *Simeon's Touch* and *The Garrity Test.*